M000210274

IRRESISTIBLE

IRRESISTIBLE

EROTIC ROMANCE FOR COUPLES

EDITED BY
RACHEL KRAMER BUSSEL

Copyright © 2012 by Rachel Kramer Bussel.

All rights reserved. Except for brief passages quoted in newspaper, magazine, radio, television, or online reviews, no part of this book may be reproduced in any form or by any means, electronic or mechanical, including photocopying or recording, or by information storage or retrieval system, without permission in writing from the publisher.

Published in the United States by Cleis Press, Inc., 2246 Sixth Street, Berkeley, California 94710.

Printed in the United States.
Cover design: Scott Idleman/Blink
Cover photograph: Eryk Fitkau/Getty Images
Text design: Frank Wiedemann

First Edition.
10 9 8 7 6 5 4 3 2 1

Trade paper ISBN: 978-1-57344-762-1
E-book ISBN: 978-1-57344-773-7

Contents

INTRODUCTION

A lot of the erotica that comes across my desk focuses on the spark of attraction when strangers meet, the cataclysmic sensation of falling, hard, for someone new and exciting. That makes sense, because there's built-in drama and erotic tension when two people discover there's intense chemistry between them. With this anthology, though, I wanted to explore what happens after that, once those people have been together a while (even a short while). I wanted to see what sparks fictional couples could produce on the page, and the results are, well, scorching.

The couples in this book explore all sorts of exciting sexual possibilities, and one of the main reasons they're able to open up in the ways they do is precisely because they have another person to rely on, coax them, challenge them, tease them and seduce them into traveling down a new sexual path. Whether that means outdoor sex, kink, a trip to a strip club or a very sensual massage, we get to see the ways the layers of trust that have been built up get used to stoke the fire that burns between them.

In addition to enjoying naughty, wild adventures, the couples here also work out differences between one another and handle issues like infidelity in ways that ultimately strengthen, rather than destroy, their relationships' longevity. In Cole Riley's "Same As It Ever Was," Joanne suspects her husband of cheating, but with a little help from her best friend, manages to recapture the sensual spirit and passion that's been missing as both husband and wife make amends and move on, knowing what it was they almost lost. Rekindling a romance that's threatened to go stale is also the theme of "Renewal" by Delilah Night, where she writes, "That touch sent a long-missing ripple through my body. I hesitated, hoping he'd remember what I love."

In "The Pact" by Elizabeth Coldwell, a woman rediscovers a man she'd once passed over, only to find that the years they've spent apart have made him someone she's sorry she overlooked. How a couple deals with a death in the family, as well as religious tradition, is the subject of "The Mitzvah" by Tiffany Reisz, as Grace and Zachary find that embracing desire can be healing. Kris Adams takes us into an African village and some complicated relationship dynamics, along with a lot of voyeurism, in "Six Eyes, Two Ears." Kay Jaybee takes a common fantasy, that of a man watching two women make love, and breathes new life into it by showing both halves of a couple as they live out this dream.

Individual characters work through their own issues with the help of their partners, getting support, love and, of course, very hot sex. "Repaint the Night," by Janine Ashbless, is about public sex, but, even more, a woman who is conquering a fear of the dark after being mugged ten years before. The erotic power of that story is heightened by Leah's awe at being able to enjoy what she and Callum are sharing, as she recovers a part of herself she lost and deepens the level of trust between them.

For those who like things a bit spicier, there's "The Netherlands" by Justine Elyot, in which a nude Loveday serves guests tea and takes orders, while fulfilling a longtime fantasy of being "used," with her true love there to watch.

Make no mistake: though these are stories about couples, they are not light or fluffy. They are full of joy, lust and kink, as well as realistic elements of mistrust, uncertainty and confusion, which the couples work through in ways that don't gloss over or ignore their differences.

These couples, however long they've been a team, push the envelope by pushing themselves to try something new, even when they're not sure where it will lead them. They go to those exotic, erotic places, to those recurring fantasies, because they know they have someone who will travel there with them. I hope this book will inspire nighttime reading—out loud—and erotic adventures, as well as conversations that have been bubbling under the surface, waiting to be exposed, just like the fantasies in the tales you're about to read.

Rachel Kramer Bussel
New York City

TWICE SHY

Heidi Champa

There is nothing like a good fuck first thing in the morning. I stretched my arms up over my head, enjoying the tired and sore feeling in the muscles of my back and legs. The deep rush of satisfaction that filled my body made me want to stay in bed, but work was calling. I knew as soon as that shower turned off, it would be time for me to get out of bed and start my day. The door to the bathroom was wide open, and I closed my eyes and listened to the sound of the pounding water, knowing it was covering his naked body.

God, we had just finished, but the thought of him soapy and wet got me going again. It was like my body had already reset, already forgotten how hard he had just made me come. I rubbed my hands over my naked skin as I listened to the water falling onto the tile of the shower floor. We had shared that small space more than a few times, and it always ended the same way, with me pressed against the cool wall and him fucking me while surrounded by the steamy spray. My fingers reached my cunt, which was already growing wet again, my desire clearly still unquenched.

All too soon, the room went silent as the pounding water came to a stop and I groaned at the prospect of leaving my warm bed. I heard him moving around inside the bathroom, but his voice surprised me nonetheless.

"You bit me."

I turned and looked at him, his torso still damp from his shower, his face fixed on the fogged bathroom mirror.

"I did what?"

"You bit me. Really hard, too. I'm going to have a bruise on my chest from where you fucking bit me."

I shook my head as I walked into the bathroom, ready to call his bluff. He turned to face me when I entered the room, his skin still slightly red from his long shower. There, right above his nipple, was a purple-red mark, a few teeth impressions visible along the edge. Damn, he was right. I *had* bit him. Scrolling through memories of the morning's activities, I couldn't remember sinking my teeth into his chest. I looked up at him, trying my best for innocence, but his expression told me I was failing miserably. I reached my hand up and ran my finger along the small oval mark I'd left on his chest. Watching his face, I waited for him to wince in pain as I pressed down on the spot, but his face didn't change one bit. His hand closed over mine, caressing my fingers with his own.

"You did it when you were coming. Right after you wrapped your legs around my back, you bit me. Pretty hard, too."

"I'm sorry, Ben. I really didn't mean to. I guess I just got caught up in all the excitement. You know I can't be held responsible for what I do when I'm coming."

"Just watch it next time, okay?"

I grabbed his face in my hands and kissed him, gently sucking his bottom lip as I finished, just the way he likes. Just for fun I added a quick nibble, but he didn't seem to mind. In fact, he turned the tables on me and grabbed my bottom lip between his teeth just for a second before pulling away.

"I promise, Ben. The next time you're fucking me senseless, I won't bite you. But, come on. Is it really that big of a deal? It's just a little bruise."

"Really? Well, how would you like it if I bit you?"

"It wouldn't bother me at all. Besides, you've left bruises on me before."

"Those were just accidents. This is different. And I don't think you'd like it at all. You've never been into that kind of thing."

"What kind of thing?"

"Things that hurt. That time I slapped your ass, you didn't speak to me for damn near three hours."

"Maybe I would like it. I know I wouldn't be a big baby about it, like you."

He smirked at me while grabbing one of my hands and pulling it toward his mouth. He turned my arm so the sensitive underside was exposed. At first, he just kissed and licked the skin above my wrist gently, teasing me enough to make my eyes close. His other hand slipped between my legs, surprised at finding me wet.

"Well, well. Does all this biting talk have you excited?"

As soon as he started rubbing his fingers over my hard clit and was clearly thinking about round two, I felt it. Ben sunk his teeth into my skin. The power of his bite took my breath away.

My free hand instinctively rose to my chest as I gasped, the shot of pain flowing through my whole body. His fingers kept swirling over my clit, but even with the deep stab of pleasure, the pain started to border on unbearable. All too soon, it felt like too much. It was at that moment that Ben released my skin, kissing the spot lightly before pulling away. He reluctantly removed his hand from between my legs and brought the moist digits up to his mouth and tasted them. He searched my face, but I didn't know what he saw.

"I guess you're right. I guess you do like it, Celia."

Without another word, he turned to the sink to finish his morning routine. I walked to the shower, still holding my injured arm close to my body. I caught his gaze in the mirror, before letting my eyes fall to the spot on his chest, which was starting to turn a little blue. Looking at my own bruise, I couldn't help but touch it. As I did, my pussy clenched, and another rush of moisture made me shudder. With one last look toward Ben, I closed the shower door harder than I needed to.

For the next several days, the little bruise on my arm consumed my thoughts. Ben was away on business, and for the forty-eight hours that he was gone, I masturbated several times, picturing his face as he sank his teeth into my skin, all the while playing with my pussy. It was shocking how much it had affected me, how such a tiny thing had taken over my mind. Upon his return, I tried to jump Ben, to get him to put his mouth on me again. But he put me off, telling me he was tired and jet-lagged. I lay awake half the night, trying to quiet the desires that were running through my head.

The next morning when I got up, Ben was already gone, leaving a note saying he had to head to the office earlier. I was officially pissed, agitated and horny as hell. I had no choice but to go to work and try and forget about that scarlet mark that was still staring up from my wrist.

All day while I was at work, all I could think about was that mark on my arm, and the throb of need that beat between my legs. I hadn't been able to stop thinking about the feel of his teeth on my arm, the concentrated sensation of the pain it produced. But, most of all, I thought about how much I liked it. I stared at the little patch of broken blood vessels and smoothed my finger over it. Resisting as long as I could, I pressed the tender little mark, shooting a dull pain through my body. It was not nearly as good as the real thing, but it was enough to get me through the day until I could get home and let Ben have his way with me, and maybe even oblige me by taking another small bite of me.

My mobile phone buzzed late in the morning, and I knew it had to be Ben. I pressed the button to pick up his call, even though I knew I should try and get some work done. As I pressed the phone to my ear, I tried to control my breathing and sound cool and collected.

"Hey, Celia. How's your day going?"

"Fine. How about you?"

"You sound a little on edge; is everything okay?"

I took another deep breath, trying to think of something sane and rational to tell Ben about why I sounded so frazzled on the phone. But I guess I hesitated too long, so he kept talking.

"I know what it is. You're still thinking about that bite mark on your arm, aren't you?"

"How did you know that?"

"I just had a feeling, after seeing your reaction last night when I said I was too tired to have sex. I can't believe that all this time, I had no idea you were into pain."

"I'm not 'into' pain. I mean, I don't think I am. All I know is I can't stop thinking about it. But it's not just about the pain. It's something else, too. Something more than that."

Ben didn't respond and I stared at the stack of work on my desk and the message light blinking on my office phone. I hadn't done one thing since I'd come in to work. I knew I would never be able to concentrate until I satisfied the curiosity that had been gnawing at me since that moment in the bathroom. I made a rash decision, talking quickly before I could change my mind.

"You know the Montclair, around the corner from my office?"

"That cheesy motel we always laugh at?"

"Yeah, that's the one. Meet me there in one hour."

I hung up before he could agree—or disagree—suddenly feeling lighter. The phone call allowed me to get through a stack of work before I had to meet Ben, so I didn't feel so guilty about taking an extra-long lunch break. Ignoring the questioning looks from my coworkers, I practically ran out of the building, not even bothering to take my car, choosing instead to walk the two blocks to the motel.

I arrived before he did, sitting in the tiny armchair that was the only other piece of furniture in the room. Taking off my blazer, I tried to remain calm as I waited for the door to open, for Ben to join me, but I was jumpy, the confluence of need and anticipation making my body nearly shake. It didn't take Ben long to arrive, his demeanor the complete opposite of mine. He couldn't have been more tranquil, and seeing him that way only made me more antsy. He had to know what I wanted, but he seemed completely unaffected by it all. He began taking off his suit, undressing without me even asking. As he slid his tie off, he gazed at the bed and its tacky floral covering. He yanked it from the bed, throwing it and the extra blanket underneath it to the floor. Looking at me, he hooked his finger and motioned for me to come closer.

"Well, what are you waiting for? This was your idea, after all."

I didn't answer him, just walked the short distance to him, shedding my blouse and skirt along the way. I had spent the whole morning thinking about this forbidden hour, visions of it pushing away all other thoughts. Pulling my panties to the floor, I stood in front of him naked, not sure exactly what to do next.

He walked over to me, pausing just a moment to set his glasses on the dresser next to him. From outside, I could hear the noontime traffic. The window was open a bit, and a light warm breeze was flowing in, making the room seem less sterile.

"So, Celia. What exactly is it you want?"

"You know what I want."

"Do I? I don't think you ever said, at least not really."

I stared at him, noticing the curl of his smirk as he finished removing his pants, leaving his hula-girl boxers in place. I loved that he wore such outlandish things under his conservative suits. His hands slid down my arms and back again, resting lightly on my shoulders. I took one last look at the mark on my arm, which was now a full-fledged bruise, and I knew I had to say it.

"I want you to bite me."

"Is that all? I mean, I already did that two days ago. And I could do that just as well at home."

"You know what I mean."

"I want you to say it, Celia. Say the words and I'll do it."

"Ben, I want you to bite me. I want to feel it while you're fucking me. I want to feel it while I'm coming. I can't wait another minute; I need it now."

The last words came out as a whisper, my eyes falling from Ben's gaze. He took my face in his hands, forcing my eyes back up.

"Get on the bed, Celia. Now."

I didn't move right away, but Ben helped me along with a playful shove, and I landed facedown. He pulled me up to my knees, his hands running over my asscheeks, raising goose bumps despite the warm air blowing from outside. I waited for the sharp blow of pain his teeth would provide, but he had more in store for me than I realized. He parted the cheeks of my ass and pressed his tongue to my puckered hole. He made one spiral and then another. The tip of his finger teased my wet cunt, entering me easily as his tongue continued to work. It all felt so good, but it wasn't what I wanted. As another finger entered me, his tongue dove into my ass, nothing teasing or gentle about it. The tip went right for my center, pushing my asshole open little by little. I couldn't stop myself from rocking back into him, trying to get more of his fat tongue in me.

But he stayed firmly in control, his tongue easing away, going back to feather-light licks around my rim. I groaned at the torture, but loved every second of it. He was groaning too, pushing his tongue back into my ass, wiggling and squirming his way deeper inside. His fingers kept up their steady rhythm, joined by his thumb strumming my clit. His mouth left my ass, his voice breaking as he spoke to me.

"Tell me again. Tell me what you want."

"I want you to bite me, Ben. Please."

His mouth grazed over my asscheek, down to the sensitive skin of my thigh. I held my breath; his fingers stopped moving inside me for just a moment as I felt it. My gasp filled the room as his teeth sank slowly into my flesh, the pain searing and direct. My pussy clenched around Ben's fingers, the slow pull and push of them starting again. He moved up my body, this time his teeth gnashing on my ass, a series of light nips mixed in with hard bites as he moved all over my asscheek with his mouth. I felt like I was going to come right there around his fingers but Ben moved again, taking down his boxers and entering me with little fanfare, sliding his cock inside me slowly.

I couldn't speak. His tongue slid over my shoulder blade, and then his teeth closed around a tender section of my skin.

He kept repeating this action, a soft lick followed by a sharp snap of pain as he bit down upon me. I gasped and sighed every time he bit me, a deep thrust of his cock joining each moment of sensational pain. My body and brain were overloaded, like I was experiencing a tiny short circuit each time I felt his mouth leaving its mark on my body. He stopped long enough to whisper in my ear, his cock still moving inside me as he spoke.

"This is what you wanted, isn't it?"

His voice was rough as he asked; my voice had nearly left me altogether, but somehow I managed a response.

"Yes. Oh, god, yes. This is what I wanted."

He gripped my brown, silky curls and pulled my head back hard. A shudder ran through me and his mouth approached my neck, his lips sliding up and down the curve from my ear to my shoulder.

"Do you want more?"

"Yes. More."

I couldn't say any more; the only things leaving my lips were sighs and moans. I felt his pelvis hit my ass, his cock inside me as deep as it would go. He held us both still, his mouth hovering close to me, his breath hot and moist on my skin. The stillness was overwhelming, but I just waited for him to do it. After I took two more deep, shaky inhales, I felt it. The pain was so pointed, so focused, it took several moments for it to radiate down and all around my body. As the pain spread out in waves, he began fucking me again, adding thick pleasure on top of the ache. When his teeth released, the endorphins they left behind went straight to my pussy, pushing me so close to the edge. His mouth moved down a few inches on my neck and repeated the process, the second bite slightly harder than the first. I rode back against him, delight and agony warring inside me, so much sensation I could barely stand it. My moans were getting louder and I knew I couldn't last much longer. Ben's voice was muffled, his lips vibrating against my skin.

"I want you to come, baby. Come all over my cock."

I opened my mouth to answer, but I was cut off, not by words but by another sucking bite from Ben. I screamed—in joy, in pain, in ecstasy I never thought was possible. My body couldn't take any more stimulation; my pussy was contracting hard around his cock. My head flew back, my orgasmic moans and screams bouncing off the cheaply plastered walls. He was pounding me with more fury and force than even my recent fantasies had allowed. I felt his sweat dripping onto my back, my own body hot and sticky. His heavy chest collapsed against me and my knees gave way, leaving only my elbows to hold us both up on the bed. His teeth sank into my shoulder gently as the last quakes rumbled through both of us.

We lay in the bed, staring up at the water-stained ceiling, our cooling bodies covered by the rough hotel sheet. The clock next to us indicated that we would soon be late, but neither of us seemed eager to move. His hand reached out and turned me toward him, his lips covering mine before I could say a thing. When he pulled back, I looked into his smiling eyes and winced a bit as he ran a thumb along the line of bite marks he had just left on me. I didn't mean to say it, but my mouth opened before I could stop it.

"Ouch!!"

Ben laughed, and I knew exactly what he was going to say.

"What do you mean, 'ouch'? I thought you said you weren't going to be a baby about it, like I was. Remember?"

Getting out of bed, I looked around for my clothes, reluctantly leaving the comfort of his arms. I met his eyes and couldn't help but smile as the words came to my lips.

"Bite me, Ben."

SAFE FOR WORK

A. M. Hartnett

It started with a text message: *I want to be fucked.*

As soon as Denise sent it, she went to the window and used two fingers to pry apart the slats in the venetian blinds.

Rex was standing by the truck with his cousin, Frankie. They had just gotten back from moving a three-bedroom house from one end of town to the other. Her husband looked no different today than he did any other day. His reddish-brown hair was licked by the wind. His beard was trimmed neatly around his full lips. His sunglasses covered his brown eyes. A plain gray T-shirt bearing the words M&B MOVING in block letters on the back and his name across the right breast in the front hugged his big upper body.

He wasn't pretty. It wasn't that he was ugly. No, he had great lines that reminded her of something out of a book on Greek mythology she'd had as a kid: straight nose, square jaw, wide forehead. He looked hard. His arms were so inked it looked like he was wearing flesh-colored gloves. His skin had been a tapestry he had kept covering with an assortment of images that ranged from the grotesque to the racy to the beautiful. Rex was about as straight and narrow as they came, but he looked like a badass and that just did things to Denise.

She stifled a giggle as she watched him reach for his phone. Aside from a slight crease between his eyes, Rex didn't register any reaction when he looked at the screen. He slipped the phone back into the holster and carried on his conversation with Frankie.

Denise stamped her foot. "God damn."

She went back to the desk and set the phone to voice mail. She took her cell and went down a narrow hall that smelled like fresh paint, into an office that was crammed with used office furniture but still tidy.

Like the reception area, Rex's office faced the driveway. She could see him through the window. He hadn't budged.

"God damn."

She sank onto the seat of his ancient green desk chair and parted her legs. Camera poised at her crotch, she reached down, pulled aside her panties and took a picture. She wobbled as she righted herself and then flopped down into the chair.

A few seconds later the word *SENT* appeared on her screen. She rolled the chair to the window and craned her neck. They had moved. She could see Frankie, but only part of Rex. She could see the holster where his phone hung from his hip.

He placed his hand over the holster, but instead of pulling it out and looking at it, he simply leaned against the truck and continued his conversation.

"God *damn!*"

She always did have a thing for Rex. For the first year after she'd taken the job at M&B, he'd been a married man. Well, a separated man headed for a divorce. The second year he'd had a girlfriend that no one in the office had liked. On the day that marked her third anniversary working for him, he'd taken her to dinner and that was that: she'd been awake until almost two o'clock in the morning with Rex sprawled and panting beneath her. They'd gotten married six months later.

As on fire as he was for her out of the office, once nine o'clock came, he was all business. Today was no different. He wore a smirk and his gaze followed her whenever she crossed his path. As he'd been leaving for the job he'd just returned from, she had reached out and touched his arm. He'd just grinned and said, "Later."

It was enough encouragement for Denise, but as far as she was concerned "later" had come and gone. It was past the lunch hour. She was dying for him, and he was doing a hell of a job making "later" stretch for hours.

The second she heard an engine start, she shot up and bolted down the hall. She walked into the front office just as Rex came through the door.

He held up his hand as he yanked off his sunglasses with the other. "Don't get too excited yet. Frankie's coming back in."

She sat on the edge of her desk and watched while he strode to the water cooler and filled a plastic cup. "You get my picture?"

He waited until he had drained the cup before he answered her. "I did, and we'll take care of that problem in a few minutes. Just go back into my office and wait for me. I'll be right there."

Anticipation coiled in her belly as she spun on her heel and returned to his office. She heard Frankie's voice, heard the bathroom door click shut, heard Rex's heavy footsteps coming down the hall. He locked the door behind him and wrapped his arms around her waist from behind.

Denise chuckled. "I don't get a kiss?"

"Mmm-mmm. This is better." He shoved his hands beneath

her pink T-shirt. "I've been thinking about your nice tits all day. I almost ducked into this lady's nice bathroom to jerk off."

"It's a wonder you can get it up at all. You got less sleep than I did."

"I got enough."

He worked the cotton cups of her bra down and rolled her nipples between thumbs and forefingers until they hardened. Denise pressed her tongue to the roof of her mouth as stinging licks of electricity raced through her body and throbbed between her legs.

He nuzzled against her ear. "Now I'm thinking about bending you over that desk, yanking down your panties and fucking you as good as I fucked you this morning."

His words bled through her as he pressed his thigh between her legs. In an instant she was simmering just beneath the surface.

She let her weight drop onto his hard thigh and shimmied back and forth, gathering heat through the layers of denim between them.

Rex groaned and pushed forward until the edge of the desk cut into her thighs.

"I'm not letting you fuck me with Frankie in the can," she said, but she wasn't entirely sure she meant it. Giggling, Denise flattened her hands against the surface.

"He'll be gone soon."

He flicked his thumbs across her nipples. Denise bit down on her tongue to hold in the moan that leapt to the back of her throat. She tried to squirm around but he wedged her against the desk. The sound of the toilet flushing jarred her but she nonetheless worked with him, wriggling as he shoved her skirt to her waist.

He slipped his hand between her legs and rubbed his knobby

fingers against the damp swath of fabric covering her pussy. "I won't fuck you until he's gone. I'll just play with you for a little bit."

As he rubbed her through her panties, Denise sucked in a deep breath and stared straight ahead at the hideous woodland print tacked onto the wood paneling behind the desk. Back and forth, back and forth, he traced the indentation of her pussy.

"Listen," he murmured. Beyond the silence of the office she could hear drawers opening and closing, keys jangling and Frankie's heavy footfall.

"Thank god," she said in a puff of breath, then sucked it back in a few seconds later when there was a rap at the door.

"Rex, you want anything?" Frankie called from the other side.

"Naw, I've got everything I need," he called, his voice even and betraying nothing.

He crooked his finger against her clit and pushed down. Denise hissed through her teeth and pushed down on the desk. As heat pooled in her belly, she moved with him and rode the hand that worked her.

The moment the door slammed, he shoved her panties to her knees. She heard the crinkle of the condom wrapper and the snap of latex. Palms flat, ass up, Denise held her breath as the thick head stretched her.

His first thrust seemed to take forever. With every inch, Denise curled her toes inside her shoes and curled her fingers on the desk. When he'd given her the whole hot length, he let out a low groan and clamped his hands on her hips.

A ripple of heat scurried through her abdomen. The muscles of her cunt clenched around his dick. Impatience bubbled up her throat and frothed at the tip of her tongue. Rex drew back so quickly she gasped from the sudden emptiness.

By the time she heard the crunch of gravel under Frankie's tires, Rex had started pumping her. Denise rocked on the balls of her feet to meet him as he dragged her backward and forward. The edge of the desk cut into the tops of her thighs and delivered a jab of pain each time he shoved deep.

"Close your legs a little," he said in a low voice that ran through her like a belt of whiskey. "I wanna feel you squeezing on me."

She did as he told her and moaned as he slowly gave her every inch. The thick head passed over her G-spot. At the same moment, he reached around her. Denise's legs started to turn to jelly as two fingers played with her clit.

"There. Right there," she said breathlessly. His fingers lingered where she was most sensitive, rubbing and smearing her juices around her swollen clit.

A small but powerful ripple went through her as he worked her. Her nails scraped the worn surface of the desk as she gripped the edge. Rex's other hand moved from her hip to the center of her back. He pushed down until her bare tits were squashed against the surface of the desk.

She went up on her toes as he pulled back. A quick intake of breath preceded the deep thrust that jolted her. The muscles in her feet, along her calves and in her abs went taut as she resisted the urge to push him off, but he bucked against her and pushed her down against the desk. His grumbling laugh surrounded her, thrilling her as much as the fucking did.

The coarse hairs on his belly rubbed against her ass, the friction making the skin hot. As if seeing into her brain like an X-ray, Rex unfurled his fist and his palm came down on her right cheek in a loud slap.

Denise pushed up. He pushed back. It was just a mockery of resistance, enough to set off that click inside that amplified the pressure of his body against hers, inside hers.

She pushed again, this time to get him deeper. He didn't say anything more but she could still feel his words running through her, bumping the ridges of her spine and popping in her blood. His feet were planted against hers, holding her open. One hand remained on her ass above the hot splotch of heat where he had smacked her.

"I know how much you like dirty. That's what I'm gonna give you all night."

He withdrew until she was merely corked. For just a moment, the absence of his hot length throbbing inside left her shaking. She felt the energy around her surge and sucked in a breath, and then it hit. Rex reared against her, pumping deep and hard.

The scent of lemon cleanser permeated from the varnished wood just inches from her nose. Her vision was limited to the ratty moss-colored chair on the other side of the desk. There was little else to do but take it, just as she knew he intended it and just as she wanted it. Her breath spurted out in shallow bursts that coincided with every pass over her G-spot. Finally a moan broke through and just kept coming. The desk beneath her wobbled and groaned. All around her was the breathless melody that exploded from both of them.

Denise's climax slammed into her, bursting outward and filling her with liquid heat. The muscles in the backs of her thighs and in her calves seized as her cunt spasmed around his dick. An amalgam of filthy words erupted from her husband as his dick pulsed and he emptied into the tip of the condom.

"Oh." She breathed the word out and rested her hot cheek against the cool desktop.

A similar sound gurgled from the back of Rex's throat as she continued to throb around his cock. She felt him losing steam like a kettle taken off the burner. The weight of his body increased as he sagged down, until his forehead rested against her back. She closed her eyes and let exhaustion take over.

A few minutes later Denise was vaguely aware of his movements behind her. His hands moved to her hips and squeezed down while he pushed himself upright and pulled out.

She was too lethargic to move, so she simply propped herself up on her forearms and watched him amble around the desk to toss the condom into the wastebasket. He yanked his jeans up to his hips and then sank into the chair.

Still panting a little, he sprawled back with a lazy grin. "That was worth the hard-on I had all day." He cocked his head and his smirk widened. "You look fucked half to death."

"That's how I feel." She struggled upright and looked around the office. Though it had felt like the room was shaking while Rex had been fucking her, everything was still intact. "I'll be right back."

A few minutes later, she emerged from the bathroom. Rex was behind his desk, feet on the surface, hands behind his head with his elbows stuck out. He grinned as she wiggled back into the room, still adjusting her panties. "Is this part of some new diet you have going? Skip lunch and burn off the calories another way?"

She shook her head, then leaned against the doorjamb and fluttered her lashes at him. "I'm starving now. Can you go get something from the machine?"

"Wait a second." He stood and walked toward her. His hands were warm on her hips. "I think we need to talk about what just happened here."

"Do we? I'm pretty satisfied with the outcome." With one hand she lifted the flaps of his shirt up to his belly button, and with the other she stroked the trail of hair she found. "Don't even think about giving me the work-is-work and home-is-home speech. I'll just find another job, but I'll only be sending you nasty messages and pictures from across town. Then what are you going to do?"

His large hand rested on her ass, the heat bleeding through her skirt for a moment before he tugged one side up and gave the elastic in her panties a snap. He pressed her against the door-jamb. "You ever been fucked in the back of a moving truck?"

Denise felt a fresh surge of wanting as his gaze honed in on her lips. She ran her tongue across the upper and said, "God damn."

REPAINT
THE NIGHT

Janine Ashbless

L et's go out, Callum," I say. "I want to go walk in the
 hayfield."

Callum lifts his eyes from the road map, which he's been
using to work out our route home. It's our last night in the farm
cottage and we're in the middle of packing our bags. "You're
kidding me."

"No."

His eyes widen. His eyebrows were once blond, now gray;
either way they're nearly invisible. His face is growing more
inscrutable as the years perversely refuse to line it. "Are you...
sure?"

"I want to try it."

Quietly he nods. There are a hundred things he could say,
but he holds them all back. I love him for that.

We collect light fleece jackets, but they're not really needed
because the night is mild despite the gentle breeze. From inside
the kitchen it looks pitch black out there. Callum opens the door

and holds out his hand for me. I grab on, holding him tight as we move outside.

In ten years, I've not once been outside in the dark on my own. Not to catch a bus or visit the mailbox on the street; not even to push the bins down to the end of the drive for collection. We keep the car in the garage and I access it from the side door into the house: I can drive out to places on my own, but I can't step from the safety of the driver's seat once I've parked unless there's someone friendly there to meet me. Even that makes my pulse race and my skin crawl. Now, right now, with my hand in Callum's firm grip, I can feel the night sniffing at me like a great black beast wondering whether to take a bite. I feel it tasting me, the flutter of the night breeze like the lap of a cool tongue on my prickling flesh.

"You okay?" he murmurs.

I nod, not answering.

"Tell me if you want to go back."

"I will."

It's not so dark though, as it looked from inside. And as soon as we step away from the house and let our eyes adjust, the landscape around us starts to emerge dimly. This is late May, not a black midwinter night: even at eleven there is a faint glow in the sky, and the stars look fuzzy. The moon has risen, backlighting the clouds, and the dark cutouts of the hills and hedgerows are silhouetted against the paler backdrop of the heavens. From the corners of my eyes, I can make out more: the webbed outline of the folded clothes pole, the humps of garden shrubs, the glimmer of that kitsch concrete sundial in the middle of the lawn.

I can smell the night-flowering stocks planted under the kitchen window and I breathe the perfume gratefully, embracing it with my body. We walk across the grass, hand in hand, past the apple trees to the stile at the bottom of the garden. "Careful," says Callum, as he helps me over.

We found the hayfield on the first day of the holiday, when we went out exploring along the network of footpaths that leads out across the fields, down into the valleys and up through the woods and the disused quarry and eventually, over two miles away, to the village. Our hired cottage here in the West Country is beautifully isolated down a sunken lane, our nearest neighbors scattered and hidden away in folds of land. During the day we can hear the occasional noise of a car passing and sometimes the lowing of cows in the hills, but we're not overlooked by anyone and most of the countryside is a patchwork of arable land—grass on the steep slopes, maize in the valley bottoms, blue-green sweeps of growing wheat and brilliant yellow acres of oilseed rape—so it's quiet except for the birdsong. We love it. We walked for miles, and drove out every day to visit the coast and the little towns and the blustery moors for further walking.

The first field beyond our garden fence is all grass, left tall and ungrazed, and slopes down to the hedge of tall hawthorn and oak trees at the bottom. Yellow wildflowers grow here and there among the feathery purple seed-heads of the grass. In the dark I can't make out any colors, but I can feel the soft brush of the hip-high grasses through my thin skirt, and just make out the dark line of the path that cuts through that pale pelt. I've got to be careful with my footing here, not like on the mown lawn; I walk close in Callum's footsteps.

There's a picture of this meadow over our bed in the cottage. I recognized the shape of the clustering hills, but there the naturalism ends. The grass is painted in fiery, aching reds and purples, as if it's burning.

That first day here, in the middle of the afternoon, Callum took me in his arms and nuzzled up against me. "I should lay you down here in the meadow," he growled, "and have my wicked way with you. Bring you home all pink and happy and stuck with grass-seeds."

I giggled and pressed up against him, then was impressed to find it was not entirely a joke on his part: there was a semi-hard erection stirring already in his jeans. The spring sunshine, I reasoned; the start of a week off together. The isolation. "I don't think the farmer would appreciate us flattening his hay," I pointed out, as Callum kissed my throat.

"Mmm..." He gripped my hips, pressing both thumbs just above my pubic mound, making me squirm deliciously. "You'd love it, Leah...."

I would love it, he was right. Well, part of me. I was excited by the thought of the freedom and the impropriety, but too much of me was self-conscious. "Don't be silly," I giggled. "We're overlooked here."

"What?" He nibbled at my earlobe. "There's no one in miles!"

"There's a bridle-path up the hill there, under the trees. We could be seen." I pushed him away. "Save it for the bedroom, Romeo."

Callum sighed and bumped me against his crotch. "You're wasting a magnificent opportunity here, you know," he said, his lower lip thrust out boyishly.

I patted his stiffy in consolation, allowing myself a greedy fondle of his ball sac. "And it'll still be magnificent when we get back to the cottage. I promise."

"You expect me to walk that far with *this*?"

"For *this*," I answered, pulling his hand down to cup my sex and speaking with my lips brushing against his, "Yeah, you'll walk that far."

"I'd walk to the fucking moon," he admitted.

That was in broad daylight. Now, in the dark and nearly a week later, we stand in the same field and there's no levity, no teasing. Sweat is crawling down the small of my back and my heart is smacking like a clenched fist against my breastbone. The night circles me and I hear its eagerness in my own shallow breathing. It's only Callum's warm grip that's stopping the great dark beast from sinking its teeth into me.

For ten years I've been scared of the night. I close the curtains at twilight. I sleep with a bulb on in the hall and the bedroom door wide open. I won't open the front door at all after dark.

Isn't ten years too long?

Isn't it *enough*, now?

"Callum. Just stop there."

"Okay?"

I circle round in front of him, using him like an anchor point, and reach up to touch his face. Tight, spare flesh on his bones. A soft bristly mat of hair, all silver in this moonlight. "Just stay still, will you? Don't speak." Then I turn away and step out into the sea of grass, and I'm no longer touching him and all I can see is the night.

Ten years ago—more now—I was walking home through the park, and it was November and it was dark. Callum didn't like me coming back home that route, not on my own, but I wasn't afraid in those days. Nothing bad happened in our part of town. Nothing bad happened to us. I was almost home, actually in sight of the last road I had to cross, when from under the shadow of a tree someone stepped out behind me and grabbed me. He shoved me to the ground, bouncing my face off a rock. He wrenched the bag off my shoulder and he ran.

That was all. I should be grateful, shouldn't I, that it wasn't worse? My cheekbone was broken and I still have the scar where the stone cut my skin, but it's not really that noticeable. It could have been so much worse. I ought to have shrugged it off and gotten over it, I tell myself—but I didn't. My fear of the night grew thick and wild, out of all proportion.

The terrible thing is that I heard him. I heard the scuff of his feet as he stepped out, heard the rasp of his breath at my back. And I didn't react. I didn't even break into a run; I couldn't think fast enough. I just kept walking, like ignoring it would make it not happen.

For ten years I've hidden from the night. At first I was ashamed of my fear, but shame doesn't make it go away and neither does stumbling helplessly onward. Now, in this field, I stand still. And I let the night catch up with me.

The silence is vast, like the gape of jaws. It makes me feel tiny. No birdsong now, not even an owl. No traffic noise out here. Only the soughing of the breeze in the trees and—yes, there: the faint rumble of a plane miles overhead, right at the limit of my hearing. That breeze is just cool enough to raise my nipples to hard points under my clothes. I lift my breasts, filling my chest with that air, trying to keep my breath slow and even. The night smells clean and my nipples tingle, like stars. The skin between my shoulders prickles. I can feel Callum's gaze upon me; I know he's right there, though I can't see him. He's right there at my back, like the man under the tree was, like the night is: ready to seize me.

My hands are shaking as I lift them to the zip of my fleece. My eyes are wide, searching but blind. There's nothing to see except the dark. Hands tug, the zip gives way. I cast the fleece aside. With ungainly movements I stoop and snatch up the hem of my dress, peeling it over my head. I hear the catch of Callum's breath and gooseflesh explodes all over my shoulders, but he says nothing. The empty air embraces my waist and my thighs like a caress. My breasts feel huge and heavy in the night's cool hands. My nipples rasp on the lace of my bra. Two straps—a hook—that's off, too, thrown aside. My breasts bounce free. I spread my arms wide, letting the dark lick me all over. It's very nearly as much as I can bear.

"Callum!" My fingers curl beseechingly.

He's there, watching out for me. He steps up behind me and I shudder as he slips his hands around me and cups my breasts. I feel my nipples, stiff with fear and chill, jutting between his splayed fingers, and I arch in his embrace, writhing with both delight and terror. His breath is hot in my ear.

"Leah. Oh, god..." The voice is hoarse, not his, not his alone—it is the night speaking through him, strained and eager. He pinches and tugs at the points of my breasts, making all their round vulnerable warmth the captive of his hard hands. I feel a sudden gush of heat in my sex, and I press my ass back into his groin, finding the abrupt jut of his arousal.

"You're fucking beautiful, Leah," he groans. He only swears when he's really turned on. Reaching one hand to his groin, he scrabbles frantically at his clothes. I feel the bite of his fly buttons against my cold bottom. Then the burning slat of his cock slaps on my cheek, rubbing up against me. He growls my name again, in my ear, and fumbles at the lace of my panties. "Want you. Want to..."

Fingers tug down my last garment, exposing me. They push into the furrow of my sex, spreading, and the night rushes in to tongue the wet flesh between. My whole body is quivering. I feel the surge in his cock as he realizes just how slick and juicy I am, and the press of his flesh makes me want to open for him and enfold it in my thighs. My mouth is making little broken gasping noises, but I manage to find one whole word: "Wait!"

His grip slackens. I slide out of it, knees folding, down the length of his torso and his legs. His belt buckle scores my back.

His cock tangles in my hair and butts my turned cheek, planting its own wet kiss. Then I tip forward onto hands and knees, presenting my raised ass, bowing to the earth. My upthrust cheeks must glimmer in this light. I hear him wrench off his fleece and shirt, swearing under his breath with awe and impatience. Grass folds beneath my forearms and soft seed-heads tickle my belly. The smell of crushed greenery is sharp but I can smell myself, too, the heavy aroma of my arousal. I want him to grab me quickly, before I panic. I want him to mount me from the rear as I press my scarred cheek to the earth, among the flattened stems.

Instead, he does something he has never done in the safe and cozy confines of any house, nor in all the years we've been together. The night must have granted him permission; he kneels and grasps my ass and pushes his face into the cleft between my cheeks, his tongue wet and squirming on my butthole. The shock makes me squeal. Hot and cold flashes erupt through my flesh, and suddenly my fear of the dark isn't uppermost in my mind. A warm wet tide sweeps me off my feet. He lifts me so he can press lower, raking the split of my sex with his mouth, but returns to the forbidden pucker, snuffling and sucking and thrusting with pointed tongue until the clench gives way and he's forced my surrender. There's this *sensation*, one I can't name. If it had originated in my clit I'd call it an orgasm, but it comes from my anus so I don't know what to call it, this tumbling thrill that cascades out from the darkest part of me, turning to light as it goes so that my fingertips blaze incandescent. I cry out, muffling my face in the cool grass, and start to sob.

I'm crying his name.

I'm just crying.

Callum lays me down on my side. He knows me well enough not to be afraid of my wild noises. I feel him kneel over me, am dimly aware of him stripping his shoes and jeans off, and then he scissors in between my thighs, his beautiful big cock that I love so much nudging its head up against my pussy, demanding entrance into the warm, wet depths. I open gratefully to its thick girth.

"Shush, love," he tells me. "It's okay."

We're naked together, fucking in the grass, in the night, in the dark.

From here I can see the grass dancing above me. I can look up and see the stars outlining Callum's head, the shimmer of the moonlight on his pale hair and glistening brow. He sinks his left thumb into my folds, rolling my clit, and with his other hand he gets a good grip on my hip. I can see the jet-black outline of an oak canopy waving in the breeze. The hiss of the wind is all around me. The night is alive with movement. It surrounds us, poised.

I can feel my body opening up to him as his cock moves inside me. But not just opening to him. *Take me,* I whisper silently as his thrusts spread me wide: *Come into me. I want you. I need you. Fill me. Eat me. Fuck me. I need to be fucked. I need to have you inside me. I need the dark. I need the night.*

The night hears me. Callum reaches out and shoves his thumb into my mouth, wetting it on my tongue. He takes this wet back down, out of my sight, up into the split of my cheeks. There's not much room between us but he gets a hand in somehow. He circles the moist digit about my ass, probing the softened hole and then working it inside me. My body experiences again the invasion and the terror and the yielding, the burning surrender. And all the time, Callum is drumming my clit and slapping hard up between my thighs, and I feel all the fear melt into something just as merciless, just as overwhelming. His shoulders stiffen as he sinks deeper, thrusts harder, leaning into me. His face is shadowed, the moonlight not touching it: I am being fucked by a man of darkness. I can hear the rasp of his breath—but this time it is not over my shoulder; this time I am twisting to face him and clutching at his hard body with my hands, pulling him into me, and he is coming hard and fierce, with explosive gasps.

And I let the whole of the huge and terrible night—with its wind and its darkness and the sighing trees, the stars and the cold—pour itself into me and take me for its own.

There. Callum and I have begun to remake my memories. Their landscape is the same but we have painted them in a different palette: the hues of desire instead of the cold blues and blacks of fear. Maybe once is not enough, but it's a start. As we walk hand in hand back to the cottage the night is crazy with color, and I'm smiling.

SAME AS IT EVER WAS

Cole Riley

It was one of the worst winters the city had ever endured. More than three feet of snow fell in less than a day and more was to come. Many businesses were closed, classes were canceled and all but the essential city services were on a forced holiday. It was cold as hell.

Joanne didn't have to go to her speech therapist job at a charter school on the city's Lower East Side because many of the streets leading to work were completely covered with snow-drifts, concealing a thick sheet of treacherous ice underneath. That was not the case with her husband, Wayne, the head of the publicity department for a large record company. His wife couldn't understand why he didn't call the company and say he couldn't make it due to the nasty weather.

"I can't do that because I've got to finish the paperwork on the DJ Burn publicity tour," Wayne said, taking off his pajama top and glancing again at the alarm clock. "If I don't go in, the work won't get done, and something could go wrong when he tours in Berlin and Munich next week. Gotta go in."

"Can't somebody else go in for you?" she asked, trying to find another way to keep him home. "There must be somebody closer to the city that could go in. I don't understand why every time there's some kind of crisis, everything falls on you. They don't pay you enough for this kind of loyalty."

"Joanne, it must be done," he said, going into the bathroom.

Irked by his dedication to a job that didn't pay nearly enough for him to go in during a blizzard, Joanne walked to the bathroom doorway and stood, watching him shave. Then he would shower quickly and drive to the parking lot to make the 8:10 train to Penn Station. Why was he so eager to go to work? Maybe he couldn't stand being with her anymore. Maybe it was something else. Maybe it was his new, pretty secretary. She'd spoken to the wench on the phone and didn't like her easy, casual manner. The woman was too friendly for her own good. How was she with him? Maybe there was something going on with the two of them.

Yes, he seemed to work a lot lately and when he got home, he was usually too tired to do anything. In so many ways, she was bored with marriage, ritual and routine.

But it wasn't always like that. During their first year of dating, she told Wayne that she loved him as much as she could. Maybe it would deepen as time went by. In those days, she had one man after another. She built a reputation for making men suffer, but it didn't chase him away. He only wanted her more.

Back then, she got off sexually on exhibitionism, showing her ass in public, fucking in public places, anything weird, and nothing but those kinky things made her excited about living or loving. It was possibly an emotional rebellion against her strict upbringing in a military household. It was her mission to unleash the freak in Wayne, to loosen him up. Their dates became a series of wild parties, at private spots with over-the-top carnal activities and underground sex shows.

One Friday night, she took Wayne to an underground frolic club in the Bronx with a heavy Latino and black crowd, and the party was hopping when they arrived. She could see things were heating up through the thick haze of cigarette smoke and the overheated spinning colored lights: girls writhing to the hot tropical beat, almost naked, with their breasts exposed and skintight jeans open and guys grinding against them with their pants unzipped and their stiff dicks out in some cases. It was totally freakish. No limits, no rules.

The longer the party lasted, the more uninhibited things became. She'd always wanted to seduce and screw a man in front of an audience, to ravish him and work everybody watching into a sexual frenzy. Lots of people watching her getting hot and heavy with a man, the center of attention: this was the night for it.

During a smoldering Machito tune with a Cuban clave beat cooking in the background, she ripped open Wayne's shirt, popping the buttons, and started sucking his nipples. Drunk on rum, he closed his eyes and let her have her way. She wanted to hurt him with desire. She pressed her lips to his chest, tasting his male scent of sweat and cologne, listening to him softly murmur his joy at having her in his life.

A wave of gasps and sighs went through the crowd when she kneeled and undid his pants, removing his dick. It was completely hard, sticking straight up. She wondered what it would be like to be a man with a throbbing erection like his, about to pop. One woman yelled, "You go, girl!" The guys were cheering her on, stomping to the lusty rhythms of the music. She held his brown legs, keeping him steady, and sucked him to the shouts and whistles of her audience, the network of veins thickening in his shaft as it plunged in and out between her lips.

"Oh, damn, baby," Wayne moaned at one point, his legs sagging.

She was fascinated with the carnal response of the people watching them, faces in ecstasy; their anguished expressions of near release and bliss. The sexual animal in them stirring with undisguised lust. The women watched imagining they were her, and the men watched wishing they were him. Some of them were now kissing, feeling each other up or masturbating openly. She begged Wayne to enter her right there on the dance floor, throw one of her legs over his shoulder and penetrate her to the hilt.

The clapping reached a peak when he started trembling, shooting his seed into her mouth, his thighs almost totally enclosed around her bobbing head. Totally aroused, she was sopping wet. She lifted a leg, took off her soiled panties and tossed them into a ring of excited Latin guys. One of them caught the underwear, yelling and pumping his fist in the air. He howled once more and covered his face with the drenched panties.

Finished, she waved and walked off the dance floor side by side with her lover. Wayne almost left her after that. To this day, he'd never mentioned that decadent night. It was as if it had never happened—but somewhere deep down, she knew it had.

Her memory of one of her wildest nights slowly faded, and she was back in her sterile married life. "Are you sure I can't convince you to stay home?" she asked cheerfully. "We could stay in bed like we used to do, eat snacks, read to each other and fool around. A day alone with just the two of us. No distractions."

He was stubborn. "No, baby, I've got to go and that's that."

As soon as her husband closed the door, she prepared the coffeepot for the two cups that would get her through the morning, the brew's rush a necessity for her sanity. She weighed the events of the day so far, fixating on his insistence on going to work. It added up to bad news.

She quickly called her best girlfriend, Francine, and asked her to drive over. Francine begged her to tell her what was wrong but Joanne wouldn't give her an answer over the phone. Three hours later, after a hair-raising drive on frozen city streets, her buddy arrived, cold and shivering.

"So, what's up, girl?" Francine asked, watching her friend over the rim of her cup. Francine was an attractive plus-sized woman who loved good food, good gossip and good sex. Her best assets were her ample breasts, cute face and saucy lips.

"Wayne's fooling around." Joanne said it like it was a fact.

"Honey, you've got to be kidding me," her friend gasped, putting down the cup. "How do you know he's cheating? Did you catch him?"

"No, not yet, but I've got a feeling that something's going down with him and his perky little secretary. I don't trust that hussy as far as I could throw her. She always answers his phone with this snide little nicey-nicey thing in her voice like she knows something that I don't know. She's all up in his business, girl. Whenever I call there if he has to work late, she answers the phone like she's the damn wife and I'm nobody. She runs his life. Whenever I get flowers or gifts from him, it's usually her that buys them. I can't stand her."

"Is that all you've got on him?"

"No, he's just different, acting different," Joanne said. "It's like he's in love."

"Well, I know you told me that you were having problems in the bedroom. Maybe that's what's got him crazy. Maybe he's having a midlife crisis."

One weekend, in a fit of anger Wayne had called her frigid when she wouldn't give him any. Frigid, hell! Her aunt told her there was no such thing as a frigid woman, just men who didn't know what to do in the bedroom. Lousy lovers. Some of it might be her fault, maybe not. One thing she'd never admitted to anyone, even to herself until a few months ago, was that she refused to give any man sexual power over her. She wouldn't let any man control her with his dick: no, sir.

"How do you tell a man that you're not being satisfied?" Joanne asked aloud. "No man can handle that. Their egos are too big to hear that."

"I guess, but I don't have that problem," her friend replied. "Henry does the best he can, and I love him, so I work around it. With him, if I didn't play with myself during sex, I'd never have an orgasm. And there's toys. That's okay with me; there's more to our relationship than sex."

Bullshit. Joanne was not hearing any of it. She was determined to catch them in the act. The cheaters. She figured that they would slip up on a day like today, with no one in the office. Her proposal to Francine was to drive into town and watch them, follow them and see what they did. Everything would be revealed.

"Drive all the way to the city in all this snow so you can snoop on them?" Francine exclaimed. "You've got to be kidding, girl. You're out of your mind. Don't be crazy."

Crazy or not, near lunch time, the two women found themselves parked a half a block from the office building where Wayne worked, sitting in a cold car, shivering. Twice during the drive there, they almost skidded off icy roads and nearly turned back, but Joanne was determined to get there to see what she must see. She was obsessed with catching her husband in the wrong. They would start the engine every twenty minutes and let the car warm up before they switched it off again. The hours passed slowly, and they waited and waited.

Finally, they saw the pair, Wayne and his secretary, come

out of the building, their heads bent down to keep the howling wind and blowing snow from assaulting their faces. As they reached the corner, Joanne ordered her friend to follow them, slowly and carefully. Their car eased along at a creep, keeping their prey in sight until they ducked into a fancy bar two blocks from their job.

Joanne suddenly jumped out of the car and ran recklessly across the street, with Francine trotting breathlessly behind her. The two women stood outside of the bar, watching the couple sitting at a cozy table, laughing and drinking.

"See how close they're sitting to each other," Joanne shrieked. "Don't tell me he's not doing her. I know he's screwing her. I've seen enough. I knew it, I knew it. Let's go."

Back in the car, Joanne continued to rant about how much of a dog her husband was, now caught in the act.

"I'll let him have it when he gets home tonight," she shouted. "I won't let him make a fool out of me with that slut. I can play rough, too."

"But is that little scene at the bar enough to break up your home?" her friend asked. "Don't you think you're jumping to conclusions here?"

"Hell, no," Joanne retorted. "I saw what I saw and that's enough for me. Take me home. I want him out by the weekend. Gone. I'll call his lying, cheating ass as soon as I get home. Don't mess with me. He doesn't know who he's fooling with here. Him and that little whore."

"What is this really about, Jo?" Francine asked. "Is this guilt? Is this about your little thing with your boss a few months ago? Is your conscience finally catching up with you?"

"No, that's different. I didn't rub his face in it like he's doing to me. He never even knew I stepped out on him. I kept everything cool."

Her affair. Her three-month affair with Michael, her boss at the school. A thirty-year-old brother from Philly with a durable runner's build who spoke fluent Chinese, Russian, French and Italian. Dark, tan and fine. She recalled her breasts hanging over her lover's face and his teeth biting her nipples hard, then harder. That almost made her hit the roof. She felt comfortable with him sexually, something she had never experienced with any other man. He complimented her on her smooth, soft behind, her long legs, and graceful swan-like neck. Called her a real thoroughbred. He held her legs up high off the bed and kissed and lapped her lower lips until she screamed and made him stop. She wanted his dick and that alone. He'd thrust solidly into her body, with her hanging half off the bed, her head almost banging against the floor. She loved the sheer male power of him.

They made love in all kinds of positions, with their bodies in all manner of contortions—against the wall, on the floor, on the sofa, against the sink, on top of the kitchen table, in the shower, even out on the balcony in the night air. She couldn't get enough of him. Many times she'd start dressing, complaining that it was getting late and that she was expected home, but he'd lift up her skirt, either to kiss her between her legs or to insert a finger. And after that, it was back to bed. Once they finished, they lay there panting and laughing.

Sometimes he'd eat her or suck one of her breasts hungrily while she called home to tell her husband that she'd be late. Working. Paperwork. Calls to make and last minute odds and ends to clear up.

Before they drove away from the scene, Francine suggested that they wait and watch what the couple did next. When the supposed lovebirds came out of the bar and returned to work, she asked Joanne if she wanted to go up and really check out what they were doing in that empty office, all alone. Her friend agreed at first but thought better of it upon further reflection. She knew her friend had always been extremely jealous and distrustful of her husband, to a fault.

It was her Achilles' heel, her blind jealousy. It was irrational, powerful and the controlling force in her emotional makeup, something she'd fought during all of her relationships—a tendency to believe the worst of any man. Now, when Joanne had the chance to actually see the truth for herself, she balked, wondering what would happen to her if all of her suspicions were confirmed.

Francine, saying nothing, got out of the double-parked car and crossed the street again. She walked right past the security guard, who quickly asked her to sign in before going up. The signature only took a moment and then she stepped into the wood-paneled elevator for the ride to the tenth floor and Wayne's office.

Quietly, she walked down the long hallway, looking for the sign that would tell her that she was in the right place. Halfway down the corridor, she located the door and gently worked the knob until it opened. There was nobody in the office that Francine could see upon entering, but the faint sounds of someone deep in the throes of hot sex caught her ear after a few steps. She tiptoed toward the song of sex, silently easing open the door that was slightly ajar and peered in shock at the sight of Wayne pounding frantically into the wetness between the secretary's outstretched legs, her head thrown back, eyes closed and hips swaying into his hard thrusts. Thank god Joanne had decided not to come up.

Francine tried to avert her gaze from the shameful sight but couldn't. Instead, she found herself standing there in the doorway, unzipping her jeans and massaging herself as the moans and sighs reached an unearthly pitch. Soon she was engulfed in sexual heat and her legs buckled. How could Joanne let some hussy like this girl get her mitts on a gorgeous hunk of male flesh like Wayne?

As the pair of lovers eventually sagged against each other after a big orgasm, lost in the blissful fog that comes after climax, she stepped back and walked silently out of the office.

"Girl, they weren't doing nothing but talking and working on some damn account," Francine lied after returning to the car and her anxious friend.

"Really?" Joanne couldn't believe it.

Francine wasn't finished. "But I think something could happen with them unless you step in. Don't be hasty. You can keep him with no trouble. All you have to do is take care of business between the sheets. Give him an erotic evening he will never forget. You've got a good man and there's no reason for you to throw him out so some woman who doesn't deserve him can get him."

"So they weren't doing anything?" She just knew he was cheating.

"Nothing at all. It was all business."

"You think I'm crazy for coming out here like this, don't you?" Joanne asked. "Tell the truth."

"No, not at all. But listen to me. You've got to stop being so self-centered, so selfish. You've got to think about somebody other than yourself. Let that man know that you want him, that you love him. Jo, I'm just saying that you should pay more attention to him at home and then you won't have to worry about a thing," Francine said, keeping a straight face. "Not a thing. Turn him out, girl. Rock his world and he won't look at another woman."

"What should I do?" her friend asked, admitting that it had

been too long since she'd put together an evening of romance and seduction. "I'm out of practice, Fran. Give me some tips."

The women stopped to pick up champagne, scented candles, lotion and bath oil. After Francine went home, Joanne prepped herself for her man's return and when she heard his key in the door, her heart raced. He called to her once to announce his arrival, then took off his galoshes and heavy coat. His voice was cheery and upbeat.

"Hello, sweetheart," Joanne said, walking sexily into the room, carrying an ice bucket with a bottle of champagne peeking out. "I missed you all day. I'm so glad you're home, honey."

He looked at her with a quizzical expression, standing up to give his customary smooch on her cheek. Then he noticed what she was wearing, a new red silk gown with thin spaghetti straps and a low, tempting V-back. Absolutely nothing underneath, from what he could see. As she walked toward him, he enjoyed the enticing jiggle of her breasts under the silk and sensed his dick jump in anticipation. He also felt a moment of extreme guilt, a flashing image of his secretary wiggling underneath him, but quickly defeated it when his wife stepped closer and placed her warm arms around his neck. Her sizzling kiss, all lips and tongue, made his privates stiffen.

"What is this all about?" he asked. "What naughty thing have you done?"

"Nothing." She smiled weakly, passing him a glass of the bubbly. "I thought we should have a nice, romantic evening for once. We don't have enough of them. I feel like I've been neglecting you lately and I want to correct that, starting tonight."

"I'm game," he agreed.

His mouth met hers before she could get out an answer, and he led her to the bedroom, where his lips and tongue did their bewitching alchemy on her breasts, neck and inner thighs. Her senses were excited beyond limit, toward an all-consuming desire that kept her coming and coming. After she reciprocated by nipping the swollen knob of his engorged dick, she screamed that she couldn't wait much longer; she wanted to feel him inside her. They switched places on the bed, into a sort of spooning, to sixty-nine each other. Both curled up, lips upon the other's sex.

He stopped the teasing before he reached his peak and righted himself, kneeling over her, rubbing his erect tool between her large breasts, hardening it even more between them. Now overcome with desire, his wife grabbed him by the shoulder and pushed him down, her other hand firmly around his dick. She smiled when he put his tool inside her, the echoes of its throbbing deep within her. The way he made love was always so open and thoughtful, and the memory of their secret rhythms pushed her to open wider still to accommodate him farther into the back of her. It slowly became too much, both of them totally lost in the rapture of their gyrations, and then she bit his neck, giving in to the roar of the sexual storm inside her. They clung to each other desperately, their arms locked around each other's body when the burst of shuddering sensation seized them, compelling them to quiver and shout in its praise.

After the lovemaking, they lay naked on the bed, holding hands and calmly chatting. She still shuddered from the aftershocks of her orgasms, her skin glistening all over from the afterglow. He sipped from her glass, stroking her hair while watching her.

"Joanne, let's start over and recapture what we once had," her husband said, kissing her eyelids. "We're still good together. I forgive you for what you've done in the past. Your little indiscretions. I haven't been an angel myself. We've both screwed up in our own way, but that's all behind us. I love you and I want to keep what we have alive. We deserve a second chance. What do you say, sweetheart?"

Somehow it didn't matter that Wayne knew about her affair with her boss. It didn't matter that he had screwed up somehow. What did matter was that he was hers again, completely hers. And nothing would change that or threaten their love again. She took his face delicately in her hands and planted one long, passionate kiss on his lips, feeling the nearness of his body give her yet another rush of desire. They held each other close all night, smug and confident in their new and improved love, and slept like babies until the alarm clock sang its annoying noise.

OUT OF CONTROL

Karenna Colcroft

The front door closed with a bang, startling Alia from sleep. *That damn door. Landlord's never going to fix it.*

She didn't really mind the sudden awakening, though. The slam heralded Reyn's return from work. This time of year, he put in such long hours they barely saw each other. If he woke her when he arrived home, it gave them time together, which didn't bother her at all. At least she might get a hug and kiss from him before he headed to his computer to unwind before trying to sleep himself.

After a moment, the bedroom doorknob clicked. Alia burrowed farther under the sheet and closed her eyes, pretending to be asleep. If Reyn believed her pretense, she'd miss her affection from him, but she rarely fooled him this way.

"Hi, honey." The mattress shifted slightly as he lay beside her. "I'm home."

"Hi," she murmured.

"Snuggle with me?"

She rolled onto her side facing him, and he put his arms around her and kissed the top of her head. "You woke me up," she said accusingly.

"You mean, you weren't awake masturbating?"

Her face heated and she swatted his chest. He chuckled. Ever since she'd admitted to him a few days earlier that masturbating had always embarrassed her, he'd teased her about it. Not in a mean way, of course. Reyn was never mean to her. Since they'd met, he'd always used humor to try to help her deal with the issues she hadn't realized she had until she'd found herself with a safe man, a man who loved her unconditionally.

"I thought you always masturbate if I'm not here to help you out," he went on, laughter underlying his voice. "Isn't that what that conversation was all about a couple of weeks ago?"

"That conversation was about me trying to write a masturbation scene in a story," she corrected. "As you very well know."

He lightly rubbed her back. "Am I upsetting you?"

"No, you're just being a pain in the ass." She kissed him. "You tease me a lot."

"If I didn't, you'd think something was wrong." He nudged her. "Turn over. I want to spoon with you."

Slowly, she turned onto her other side. He wrapped his arms around her, and she shimmied back against him. His hard cock pressed against her ass. As she registered his arousal, he covered her breast with his hand and squeezed gently. She moaned. She'd expected only a kiss goodnight. Apparently he had more in mind.

Which didn't bother her in the least. She could sleep anytime. During the summer, the time she had with Reyn became so limited they barely had a moment to kiss, let alone fuck. She'd forgotten how many days had passed since he'd last come to bed with her, and her body responded eagerly to his advances now.

Clutching his muscled arm with one hand to keep him from holding her too tightly, she rubbed her ass over his cock.

He slipped his hand down the neck of her nightshirt and tweaked her taut nipple between his thumb and forefinger, making her jump. Laughing, he did it again, with the same result. She couldn't help laughing herself. He'd discovered how sensitive her nipples were purely by accident, and he delighted in her response when he played with her this way. To her, the tweaking and pinches almost hurt, but the pleasure outweighed the pain.

As did having Reyn take over and do what he wanted to her. She hadn't yet admitted to him how much his domination turned her on. He wasn't a dom, by any means, just far more aggressive in bed than any man she'd been with, and a submissive streak she hadn't known about had arisen in her because of it. Even though she had yet to let him take complete control—no matter what he did, she held on to at least a vestige of control, unwilling to give it up entirely—knowing he would if she allowed it turned her on.

He nipped her earlobe and squeezed her breast more firmly. She gasped and writhed against him, not sure whether she wanted him to play more with her breasts or touch other parts of her body; not really caring what he did, as long as he didn't leave her in this state. She'd already been horny before he'd walked through the door, and now her clit throbbed and her pussy moistened in preparation for the fucking she hoped he'd give her.

He took his hand out of her nightshirt and ran it down her side to her thigh. She shivered and moaned again. Teasing her, he rubbed her ass, then brought his hand over her hip, not quite touching her pussy. "Are you wet?" he whispered into her ear.

"Find out for yourself." She grabbed his wrist and tried to

move his hand where she wanted it.

He shook his head against her back and grasped her hip, nuzzling her neck. His teeth grazed her skin in just the right spot, and she cried out. Just being in the same room with him turned her on. His touch pushed her arousal to the boiling point.

She wanted him. Wanted his cock pounding into her, fucking her so hard the bed banged against the wall. Wanted his hands on her body, his fingers playing between her asscheeks as she rode him. Wanted anything he would give her, but she was damned if she'd ask for it. She knew if she begged, he would fuck her hard and fast. Hearing her need always drove him to take her that way.

Even though she wanted him to take her, the game wouldn't work nearly as well if she started pleading with him this soon. He'd have to work for it.

His finger skimmed the top of her panties. Again she tried to steer his hand down to her clit, and again he refused to let her. Instead he teased her by tickling the skin just above her panties. She tried to pull away from him, and he tightened his other arm around her, holding her in a near headlock so that he forced her head back against him.

For just a moment, she thought she might choke, an instinctive reaction that she quickly quieted by reminding herself that Reyn would never truly hurt her. She relaxed and discovered that although she couldn't move her head, he didn't have his arm tight enough to prevent her breathing.

Panting, she closed her eyes. In that position she could see nothing other than the window and seeing nothing at all heightened the sensations of Reyn's touch. His hand roamed from her pelvis up underneath her nightshirt to caress her breasts again. He squeezed so tightly she cried out.

"Am I too rough?" he murmured.

"No."

"I didn't think so." He tweaked her nipple, laughing when she jumped again. "I can't be too rough with you, can I? Or at least, you'd tell me if I was."

"I'd tell you," she whispered. She didn't mind a little roughness, though. Not from him.

He let go of her and nudged her to sit up. When she did, he knelt beside her, grabbed the hem of her nightshirt and yanked it off over her head. Tossing it aside, he gazed at her with lust-lit eyes. "That was in the way. Now I can see your gorgeous tits. And now I can do this."

Bending, he closed his lips around one of her stiff nipples and sucked hard on it. His hand kneaded her other breast. Discomfort and pleasure went to war within her, and her pussy clenched in arousal.

Only the flimsy fabric of her panties separated her wet cunt from his cock now. She started to slip them off, but he grasped her wrist and lightly bit her nipple. A protest squeaked from her throat. "Not until I tell you," he growled. "I have plans for you tonight."

A thrill ran through her, caused by both his tone and his words. She barely restrained herself from asking what kind of plans he meant. He probably wouldn't tell her, and she didn't want to know in advance. Most of the time, their lovemaking was predictable. On occasions like this, when he wanted to surprise her, wanted to be in control, she'd learned to wait and see what happened. Anticipating the unknown was so much hotter than knowing what to expect.

With his hand and mouth on her breasts, he lowered her onto her back. She tried to pull her pillow under her head, and he snatched the pillow away and threw it on the floor. His free hand cupped the back of her head instead, relieving the strain on her neck without allowing her actual comfort.

He switched breasts, sucking and nibbling now on the opposite nipple. He slipped his hand inside her panties, and she let out tiny sounds of pleading arousal, asking him without words to touch her this time. His lips curved into a smile, and he dipped one finger into her wetness.

His finger grazed her swollen clit and she hissed in a breath. "Oh, you are wet!" he said, sounding pleased.

"Yes," she whimpered.

Watching her face intently, he slipped his fingers along her slit. She moaned and raised her hips, trying to make him press his hand harder against her. She needed his touch. If she didn't come soon, she would scream with frustration. Only he could bring her there.

If he would stop teasing her and touch her.

He crushed his mouth against hers and nipped her lips with his own as he continued his exploration of her pussy. Two of his fingers slipped inside her to rub her sweet spot, and she arched her back to give him better access only to have him withdraw. He met her attempt to protest with a more forceful kiss, taking away her breath long enough to prevent her from speaking.

She opened her eyes to find him looking at her with a mix of love and possessiveness so intense it sent chills through her. With his hands, he pinned her shoulders to the mattress. "Mine." He kissed her forehead with a tenderness that stood in stark contrast to his aggression. "Mine."

"Yes," she breathed.

He rose onto his knees again and stripped off his shirt, revealing his muscled arms and chest, then his shorts, leaving him in only the boxer briefs he preferred. His cock tented the front of them, and she reached for the bulge, mouth watering at the thought of sucking him dry.

He swatted her hand away and took hold of the waist of her panties. Without a word, she lifted her hips to let him remove the garment. He yanked them off so quickly he nearly ripped them and threw them onto the floor with her nightshirt.

The only sounds in the room now were Alia's gasps and Reyn's heavy breathing as he turned her onto her side. Again he wrapped his arms around her as he had when they'd spooned. This time, though, he forced his leg between hers and rolled back, pinning her partially on top of him with her legs spread wide.

He reached one arm around her back and fondled her breast with that hand. His other hand again crept between her legs, and he slid his fingers back and forth in her wetness. Each time he brushed against her clit, she cried out. That small nub had swollen nearly to the point of pain, and her desperate desire for climax added to the ache.

"So wet," he murmured.

Suddenly he pressed his finger so hard against her clit that she had to swallow a scream. With his other hand, he pinched her nipple. She whimpered from the pleasure of finally having him touch where she wanted and the pain of his rough, strong strokes.

Then he stopped, and she moaned her disappointment. "Just a minute," he told her. He pulled his boxer-briefs down enough to reveal his hard, thick cock standing against his abdomen. "Put your hand on my dick."

She followed his command and squeezed him lightly, beginning the rhythm he liked. He gripped her wrist. "No. Don't play with me. Just keep your hand there while I get you off."

Obediently, she stopped moving her hand and relaxed it. "That's it," he murmured. He pressed his finger against her clit, and she cried out. "That's right. You keep your hand on my dick, and I want you to remember this, Alia. I want you to think about this when you play with yourself. About you pinned this way, with your hand on a man's dick. I want you to feel it when you rub your clit."

"Yes," she hissed, not sure and not caring whether he heard her.

He increased his pressure. Her swollen nub ached from his touch, but she didn't want him to stop. Ever. In her core, her climax built to a peak she knew would overwhelm anything Reyn had ever done to her. The sweet pain he brought joined with intense pleasure to wipe all coherent thoughts from her mind. She usually tried to avoid this place, the purely sensual part of her she mostly hid even from him. The part that would let him control her fully.

A tiny part of her mind gibbered for a moment at the realization that Reyn had taken over. With the last of her rationality, she soothed herself with the reminder that no matter what Reyn did, she was safe with him. He would never hurt her.

Unless she wanted him to.

She shuddered and let out a low moan that rose to a growl. Chuckling, Reyn nipped her earlobe. "That's right," he whispered, his breath hot against her skin. "Let go, Alia."

Her desire built even higher. Strong flame centered in her core, consuming her lower body. Every inch of her skin tingled from his touch, and she bucked against him. *Not yet*, she thought, trying to regain a modicum of control. She wanted to come for him, hell yes, but she wanted this beautiful torture to go on just a little longer first.

"How does it feel?" He pressed his finger even harder against her clit. She shouted out something that didn't quite make it to word status and squirmed against him, begging him with her movements to hold her tighter. He kissed the side of her neck.

"How does it feel to have your hand on a man's cock while he gets you off?"

She shook her head. She couldn't speak, and she had no need to. The exquisite throbbing in her cunt defied description. She struggled, and he merely tightened his arm around her and shifted the leg he'd pinned her with higher on her own leg. "You can't get away," he said gruffly. "You're stuck here with my hand in your pussy." To punctuate his point, he rubbed her clit so firmly she yelped in pain.

"Tell me if I'm too rough," he said softly.

Again she shook her head. *Not too rough.* Rough enough to cause her pain, to bring tears to her eyes. But under the pain lay such huge pleasure she refused to stop him. He'd brought her to climax before, of course, but what awaited her this time would be stronger than anything she'd ever experienced.

She whimpered and her hand clenched reflexively on his cock. He grabbed her wrist. "Just keep it there," he reminded her. "You don't get to jerk me off this time. This is all for you, Alia. Because you're going to learn there isn't anything wrong with touching yourself, and you're going to remember this every time you masturbate from now on. Aren't you?"

"Yeah," she gasped. "Oh, fuck, yeah!"

He laughed. For a moment, his finger left her clit to thrust abruptly inside her. He rubbed her sweet spot nearly as hard as he had her clit, and she writhed as an explosion built in her core. Her entire being focused on his touch and on the ache in her pussy, an ache equal parts pain and desperate desire for him to thrust his cock into her.

"Please," she whimpered.

"Please what, my love?" He returned his finger to her clit and stroked it in fast circles. "Tell me. Do you want to come?"

"Please!" she cried, unable to form any clearer words.

"Please do this?"

He flicked her nub with his thumb and finger. She shrieked, not knowing whether in pain or ecstasy, and lifted her hips to push against his hand. Taking her hint, he stroked her harder.

She screamed, and the sound combined with his touch shoved her over the brink. Her body and mind were overwhelmed with wave after wave of pleasure so intense it stole her breath. She closed her eyes tightly, tensed against complete loss of control while knowing how futile the attempt was.

She bucked and writhed, trying simultaneously to pull away from him and to move closer to him so he would keep doing this, keep forcing the climax from her. Her clit had become so swollen and sensitive now that his strokes truly hurt, and she didn't care.

She wanted more.

And he gave it to her. As she gasped and shouted through her orgasm, he kept playing with her, prolonging the ecstasy until tears streamed from the corners of her eyes.

"Look at me," he commanded hoarsely.

Breathing heavily, still shuddering with the force of the climax that hadn't yet abated, she opened her eyes and stared into his. Triumph and lust mingled in his eyes with love so strong her heart ached.

Another spasm took her, and she was unable to keep her eyes open as she screamed again. "Please!" At least she managed a real word this time. "Please, oh, god, Reyn, please!"

"Please what?" Finally he stopped stroking her and let go of her.

She flopped limply against the mattress, panting and sobbing. Until then, she hadn't realized she'd begun to cry. With his hand, he tenderly brushed the tears away. "Are you all right?"

She nodded. "Fuck."

He smiled smugly. "Is that what you want?"

"Please." Words. She needed words. "Reyn, god...please fuck me!"

His eyes lit up. Abruptly, he rolled onto his knees and stared down at her with possessive pride. He slid one hand over her skin, and she moaned another plea. "Mine," he murmured.

"Yes," she gasped. His. Only his. He'd proven that already. No one else would have been allowed to touch her that way, to pin her down and force her to climax. She would have stopped anyone else at the first slight twinge of pain.

He could be rough with her, because she knew he didn't do it to cause her pain. He did it because she enjoyed it; and because she knew he loved her, the enjoyment was heightened.

She reached up, and he took her hand and pressed it against his cheek. "I love you."

"I love you, too," she whispered.

With a grin, he released her hand. Grasping her ankles tightly, he yanked her toward him and brought her legs up against his chest. When he bent forward, she bent with him, exposing her sex to him. Despite the discomfort from having her legs bent back so far, she smiled at him. "Fuck me," she begged again.

He thrust into her, holding her still against the force of it. She gasped as his cock filled her. In this position, each move he made brushed against her still-swollen clit, bringing more pain to the overly sensitive nub.

He drove into her hard and fast, and the bed banged against the wall. No sound came from him. Teeth gritted, he stared down at her in triumph as he fucked her.

Each time he thrust, she moaned. Her body no longer knew whether it felt pain or exquisite pleasure, and her brain didn't care. All that mattered was Reyn, holding her, fucking her.

He reached between her legs and squeezed her breasts,

watching her face for her reaction. She cried out and lifted her hips, trying to fuck him harder, though in this position she had very little freedom to move as she wanted. Eyes gleaming, he took her hint and increased his pace.

Another explosion began to build in her core, and she reached for the orgasm as he continued to manhandle her breasts. The excitement of seeing his hands on her, of being treated so roughly, added fuel to her lust, and her entire consciousness focused between her legs, on the spot where their bodies joined.

His grip on her ankles tightened, and he closed his eyes. With a loud grunt, he spasmed inside her. Knowing he'd come triggered another orgasm in her, and she bucked against him.

Several times, he twitched and thrust into her, moaning. Her own climax ripped through her, taking away her breath again. She shuddered and cried out as wave after wave hit her.

No pain any longer. Only pleasure.

Finally, he let her go and dropped onto his back, panting. Trying to settle her own breathing, she curled against him, her head on his chest. He put his arm around her. "Remember this," he urged. He closed his eyes for a moment. "Next time you play with yourself, remember this."

"How could I forget?" she murmured. Her pussy ached from his use of it, and her leg muscles complained loudly about the position he'd held her in.

Oh, yes, she would remember. This would become one of her favorite fantasies. And hopefully she'd persuade him to repeat it sometime soon.

WARRIOR

Kate Pearce

W*hat the fuck just happened?*

Ava wanted to laugh at her own stupid question. This was a war zone; stuff like this happened all the time, but not to her—never to her. One minute she was yakking to Private Brandon about the crappy food at the base, and the next she was in the sand, her skin scorched and abraded by an unexpected skid across the dunes—on her face. Fierce heat blossomed behind her and she was afraid to turn her head to see what had become of the armored vehicle she and five others had been traveling in.

"Brandon, move!"

She grabbed hold of the lanky figure next to her and half dragged, half carried him over the next sand dune. No mean feat when his IOTV (Improved Outer Tactical Vest) weighed almost thirty pounds. She dumped him unceremoniously on his ass and waited until he finished coughing.

"You okay, Brandon?"

"Yeah, Lieutenant—you?"

Ava managed to simultaneously nod and spit sand out of her mouth. "I'm good. Where's everyone else?"

"Wilkinson's gone back to check."

Ava scrambled to her feet. "He can't do that by himself. Let's go. Did someone call for help?"

Hell, she didn't want to go anywhere near the choking black smoke and flames that engulfed their vehicle, but she was in command and had no choice. No one was going to survive in there for long. She covered her mouth and ran around to the other side of the vehicle, her legs trembling, and her breath coming out in gasps. Wilkinson had already dragged two of the guys out and was struggling with a third.

Ava went to help him and staggered under the dead weight of Hernandez, the driver, whose head was not only bleeding but smashed in like an eggshell. There didn't seem to be any sign of the enemy, but then there rarely was. She could only pray help would get to them before they attracted the wrong kind of attention.

Wilkinson grabbed her arm and pointed skyward where the reassuring sound of an approaching helicopter cut through the roar of the fire and the swirling sand. She nodded and pointed back the way they'd come.

"Let's get everyone away from the vehicle before it blows."

Four hours later, Ava, Wilkinson and Brandon had been cleared by the medics and were returning to their base. The three other guys remained in the hospital. From what Ava could tell from the debriefing, their vehicle had set off an IED and been thrown up in the air. She'd been sitting on the opposite side to the driver and had fallen out along with Wilkinson and Brandon. She shivered as the gates slowly opened into the small compound and she contemplated the blazing lights. If she'd sat in her usual seat, she'd be in the hospital now.

She unobtrusively hoisted the still-shaken Brandon out of the vehicle and they made their way into the ramshackle single-story building that retained the institutional air of an unused school or clinic. She blinked at the sudden brightness and made out the figures of two men waiting for them. The taller of the two men fell in behind her commanding officer, his expression grim.

Shit.

Why was she surprised he was here? Even though they weren't serving in the same unit, they still inhabited the same space. She bit down on her already blistered lip. It wasn't as though she was expecting him to break ranks and give her a bear hug, but some reaction would've been nice.

Ava stared straight at Major Ross, who studied the three of them in return. "I've got most of the details, Lieutenant. Get a good night's rest, and report to me in the morning."

"Yes, Sir." Ava saluted as he turned and left.

Wilkinson squeezed her shoulder. "You okay?"

"I'm good," Ava murmured, trying to ignore the figure looming in front of her.

"Lieutenant, can you spare me a moment?"

She raised her voice. "Yes, Captain." With a resigned shrug, she followed the man toward the sleeping quarters at the rear of the building.

He waited at the end of the hall and held the door open for her. She glanced briefly up at his face, but could see no trace of emotion.

"Thanks, Captain," she murmured, as he followed her through and maneuvered her toward another door with a piece of paper stuck to it that read FEMALE SHOWERS. He came into the room and shut the door behind him. Luckily, it was deserted, with just a hint of steam lingering and glistening on the hastily painted walls.

She blinked as he cupped her chin and stared down into her eyes.

"You okay?"

"Mike..."

He caught her raised hand as she brought it up to his cheek. "Go shower. I'll turn the water on for you."

She watched him walk away and heard the hiss of the shower, but he didn't return. After a long moment, she stripped off her combat uniform, wincing at the ache in her muscles. Despite the force of the blast, the only thing she'd really hurt was her face and her pride. She swallowed as she recalled the acrid smell of burning motor fuel. It reminded her of one of the crazy, out-of-control backyard barbecues her dad used to throw. Her throat started to ache and she thought longingly of the shower and of somewhere to hide. She grabbed a towel from the stack by the lockers and walked through the ghostly trail of steam into the shower stall.

At least the water was hot and plentiful. Ava stood under the stream with her eyes closed and just let it flow over her. After a while, she turned to find some soap and bumped up against a hard naked chest. Two strong hands came to rest on her shoulders. She couldn't bear to look up.

Mike reached past her for the soap and she stayed passively leaning against him, her forehead against his chest. His hands touched her everywhere, looking for injuries, checking her reaction to every touch of his fingers, which felt as impersonal as those of the medic in the hospital. Ava swallowed hard and let her tears fall down his chest. She shivered as his hand curved around the nape of her neck.

"Ava..."

"Touch me, Mike."

She still couldn't look at him. His hands became more possessive, cruder and more intimate, as if he wanted her to react to him. But god, she liked it, liked him owning her, making her feel something, *anything*, even if it was as uncomplicated as lust. She pressed against him and felt the hardness of his cock rise against her soft belly. He groaned and his hands slid down to cup her ass and then delved lower until he found her sex.

Ava raised her head, focused on his mouth and drew herself up on tiptoe to kiss him. His response was as direct and raw as his touch. He nipped at her already swollen lower lip, making her shudder. He drew back with a curse and smoothed his thumb over her ragged lip.

"Shit, sorry, I didn't..."

But she didn't want that, didn't want his sympathy because... She bit down on his soapy thumb and then sucked it into her mouth, and felt his cock kick up against her stomach as she drew on him.

He wrapped her in his arms and held her tight, his breathing labored and his shaft an impatient rod of heat against her skin. She deliberately undulated her hips against his and he went still. Ava held her breath, terrified that he was going to let her go, because if he did, what was she? Who was she? She slid a hand between them and tried to grab his cock.

"Ava..."

"Fuck me, Mike." She tried to pull his hair but it was too short so she settled for digging her nails into his scalp. "Don't stop, please..."

He picked her up, his hands hard on her thighs and hips as he positioned her against the cold white tile of the shower and angled his body between her legs. She cried out as he penetrated her in one swift lunge and then started to move, his hips slamming into her as she struggled to accommodate his cock. Ava wrapped her legs around him and held on, her eyes closed as he fucked her, each jarring advance and retreat the perfect reminder that she lived and breathed and *felt...*

His breathing changed and he groaned with each hard stroke. Pleasure built inside her and she teetered on the brink of embracing it. Did she want that? Did she deserve it when others were dying and suffering around her? She gasped as he grabbed her chin and made her look into his narrowed brown eyes.

"Come for me. Fucking do it."

She tried to shake her head, but his hand slid down between their wet bodies and he fingered her clit. She climaxed with a scream into his mouth and he followed her over, his come hot and deep inside her. Ava buried her face against his shoulder and just stayed put. He shut off the water, and, still holding her, stepped out of the shower. He picked up a couple of towels and kept going toward his quarters. Ava didn't have the energy to protest that it wasn't okay for her to be with him. After the events of the day, she wondered if anyone would have the nerve or the heart to stop Mike and tell him. Somehow she doubted it.

He laid her in the middle of his narrow bed and dried her off. The towel was rough and only exacerbated her already sensitive skin, but she didn't care. His short black hair was drying in spikes. He didn't seem aware of the water dripping off him. But then why would he care? He looked like every woman's fantasy. A muscled six foot two, a soldier, and a lover who knew how to draw every bit of pleasure out of her and then make her beg for more.

He leaned over her, his big hands placed on the bed on either side of her hips, and kissed her smooth belly. She trembled as his stubbled skin brushed her flesh, trembled even more as he bent his head and licked a long lascivious line from her clit to her ass and back again. His tongue flicked over her and swirled around, probing her and making her wet again. She reached down to cradle the back of his head as he made her climax, pressing him against her needy sex and enjoying his groan.

Before she even finished coming, he crawled up her and slid his tongue into her mouth, his cock inside her, and took her again, hard, fast and needy so that she couldn't think of anything but being with him, being fucked by him, being possessed by him. She wrapped her legs high around his hips and held on until he lost his smooth rhythm and simply drove into her in short sharp strokes and climaxed, bringing her over with him.

He fell forward, his face buried against her shoulder, and stayed there. Ava didn't care. She needed to feel alive and if that meant bearing his weight, she was happy to do it. Exhaustion swept over her and she closed her eyes.

Much later she disengaged herself from his arms and went to sit by the small window. Even though it was secured, she could still make out the moon and a black strip of the night sky. Even that small glimpse seemed precious now. Everything did.

"You okay?"

She turned toward the rumpled bed where Mike lay looking back at her. She tried to smile at him and rubbed her hands up and down her arms.

"I could've died today."

"Yeah. I got that." He walked across to her, his expression carefully neutral, and crouched down at her feet. "You having nightmares?"

"Not really, I'm just..." She couldn't go on. His hand came up and closed over her knee.

"You're just wondering how you escaped with barely a scratch and others in your patrol didn't."

Ava swallowed hard. "Yeah. It seems so random."

He sighed. "I don't know what to say to you. Some guys take

solace in their religion; some find other things to believe in." He squeezed her knee. "Come back to bed."

She reached down to him and he picked her up. She touched his face. "Thank you."

"For what?"

"For being here."

"I had no choice about that. I'm stationed here just like you are."

She kissed his cheek. "For fucking me then."

He frowned. "I wanted to do that."

"No, you wanted to hold me and protect me."

"Sure, but I understood what you needed. I've been there myself, you know." He kissed her nose, her forehead and her mouth. "I'd rather it was me." His sigh was ragged. "Waiting to hear if you were okay was..." He cleared his throat. "I thought about telling you to get a desk job, or fucking you until I got you pregnant—about *anything* I could do to keep you away from this. And then I realized you wouldn't be the woman I loved if I tried to change you or could control you like that."

"As if I'd let you."

She kissed him until he drew her down onto the bed and slowly entered her. She watched his face as he thrust into her, his total concentration and the faint lines of strain he couldn't conceal. When he came, he curled himself around her and whispered in her ear.

"Don't die. Don't you ever fucking die on me."

Ava closed her eyes against the anguish in his voice, knew enough not to say anything as this most private of men spilled his guts to her. She felt the same way, would die for him if given the chance. But all she could do for now was wrap herself around him and just hold him tight.

HYPOCRITES

Alyssa Turner

It's come from far away but is still audible among the hushed murmers in the crowd. "You ought to be ashamed of yourself!"

Behind the podium, I see Jacob's hands trembling as they dangle at his side. The rest of him is sturdy as a brick, like always, exuding the kind of confidence that got him where he is today. Well, not exactly *today*. There won't be any more inspirational speeches to thousands of eager voters. Today my husband eats crow, and with a sickened stomach, I will have to watch.

I want to reach out and slip my arms around his tailored waist, feed him my unwavering support intravenously and let him find strength in my embrace, but a pinky finger lurking secretly next to his will have to do.

His eyes flickering amber in the late afternoon sun remind me of the persistent guy collecting signatures on a busy street corner. First impressions of Jacob proved lasting. Success was written on his face like a road map for overachievers—steely concentration rounded out by a warm heart. Like me, he had a feverish obsession with changing what was wrong with the world. Only second-year students in the myopic confines of a liberal college town could have that kind of delusional life's goal. Together we reveled in our optimism and every cause we undertook energized us for the next.

Jacob took the fight seriously, as seriously as he took himself. Still, he was dragged into spontaneity by my artistic whims, landing us in trouble with the dean for stacking one hundred cans of lard in the entrance of the cafeteria. The stunt cost our parents a healthy fine and sliced away a bit of Jacob's dignity, but after that, they started using canola oil, making it all worth it. By our third year, he called me his secret weapon and his closest friend. When we began to finish each other's sentences, it was time to see if we were just as in sync in the fucking department.

And so things got interesting.

Jacob wasn't exactly shy; I wouldn't say that about him. Nobody that shows up at your dorm room at two in the morning could be mistaken for bashful. But Jacob seemed to restrain himself every time we were together, as if something was on the tip of his tongue, reaching from within the silence of his open mouth on mine. It confounded me the way he kept me at arm's length, grasping my shoulders, then plundered me with stolen kisses, both needing and holding me back at the same time.

He'd let his fingers fall slowly down my arms, meandering among my goose bumps until finally guiding my hands to my vagina, coaxing my legs apart with a hopeful invitation to play.

From across the bed, biting absently on his lip, he would watch me for longer than I thought any twenty-year-old could bear, studying every movement of my busy fingers slinking over creamy folds splayed before him. His patience seemed endless. And me, the star of my very own one-woman show, learning to enjoy the subtle glint in his eyes and the soft squint of focus that creased the corners.

"Don't rush it," Jacob scolded when I went too fast. I thought I was teasing him, curling my legs into the air, giving him a full-frontal view. But Jacob was teasing *me*, sadistically making me dangle on the verge of satisfaction, swollen with arousal and needful of more.

Never soon enough, his sweet calm, set on slow simmer, would erupt with jaw muscles about to explode and his eyes narrowed on me like a spear. The restraint he wore so easily was cast aside, traded suddenly for tossing me roughly onto my knees and diving into the river he watched me create. *Oh fuck, he fits me perfectly.*

"Thank you all for coming," Jacob starts, and silence rolls over the crowd. "I stand before you today to express my gratitude for your tireless efforts and steadfast commitment during this past year. It is the work of people like you that nurtures the promise of liberty in this great nation of ours." The wind whips into my hair, obscuring my view of the strained faces gathered in front of us, hanging on each sentence he speaks. Steeling myself, I wipe my face clear and stand a little more erect. I can't focus on what he's saying...no, I simply won't.

Something, anything else to do with my mind right now would be good. *When was the first time he really surprised me?*

The night he won his first city council election produced just a little bit more insight into what made Jacob tick. He stood there in front of his campaign staff, much like we do today, with a message of perseverance and a double entendre for only my ears to decipher.

"They said we couldn't do it, but when darkness obscures your way, the sun will always follow."

I grinned. No doubt, there would be a blindfold in my future that night and perhaps some revelations. After three years of marriage, I'd learned to appreciate his cues. His public persona was that of stoic dignity, yet even the highs of victory could not outdo his need for wilder thrills or render his ripened sexuality obsolete. As dedicated to his political career as he was, it would never sustain him alone.

We escaped the last of Jacob's constituents around eleven, feigning exhaustion and the intention to get some sleep. But once his shirt lay discarded on the floor and his glasses were removed, the man who few really know made his appearance. The fuzzy cuffs were already on the bed, a present from a Christmas past. I only grinned while lying there in the flouncy little miniskirt Jacob loves to fuck me in and waited for him to materialize at my side—first to restrict my sight and then to bind my wrists.

He didn't say much; at that point, he didn't need to. He was my trusted captor. No sound, no sight, just his familiar impression on the surface of the mattress, sliding into position with the promising lick of precome over my clit and the startling chill of lube in my ass. More than a finger this time inched forward between my cheeks while eager legs found his hips crisscrossed in leather straps and I imagined the harness slung low around his blunt angles, a perverse gladiator.

Hot breath on my face gave slow prelude to his tongue, meant to mark me with saliva. I arched my hips toward his and could feel his lips turn toward a measured smile on my skin. Of course, he intended me to suffer his patience. When Jacob was wanted and needed most of his days by too many people to count, he relished taking his sweet time, delighting in the reviving power of self-control.

He eased away my little polka-dot skirt to catch a full view of his two cocks dancing at my thresholds. With my legs captured firmly in his grasp, I wished I could see the concentration pumping across his forehead in that thick vein I find so very sexy. Instead, darkness compelled me to guess the exact moment that he would decide to make me scream.

I wriggled on the bed, bucking forward to no success. Only when his desire mounted high above his resolve would I first come to know what it was like to be filled, full and heavy, in both portals at once. For months prior, he had been practicing, testing my limits with a multitude of plugs and digits in preparation for that first night. His diligence had paid off.

"I cannot properly articulate the regret I have for my failure to live up to the promise of this office." That strong baritone voice, bouncing off the concrete of the surrounding buildings, is magnetic as ever, recognizable with a single word.

His words make me cringe. Jacob never broke a promise in his life. For my birthday, he promised to take me shopping and we found the most adorable twenty-something football-player type among the endless selection of eligible swingers profiled online. The anonymity of the web had provided us a smorgasbord of eager participants. Young and dumb seemed like the safest bet, with fear of recognition easily dismissed by a low aptitude for congressional upstarts. We met Brett first for a late lunch, testing the waters, then moved onward to a hotel room tucked away in an obscure suburban corporate park.

Could that evening have been more perfect? The answer came the following year after our guest list increased to two. When the allure of my birthday parties became too great to enjoy only once a year, we secured a discreet apartment downtown for the sole purpose of hosting such gatherings as often as we could.

* * *

"Though my marriage remains intact, the embarrassment my actions have caused is insurmountable, and I publicly apologize to my cherished wife of eighteen years."

In the back of my mind, I knew it was risky, but asking a new playmate to the apartment seemed like a good idea at the time. Precautions are important; Jacob was adamant about that and there was no way he'd have approved of a last-minute addition. Still, Lyle's profile picture was so fucking beautiful, I just couldn't resist when the request to meet appeared in my inbox. Forwarding his health screening even before I asked was like icing on the cake. He was clean, cute and looking for a new experience—harmless enough.

From the moment I woke that morning, the hours stretched out before me with no concern for my itching anticipation. I was a giddy bundle of nerves and excitement and I purposely didn't call Jacob the whole day, fearing he would know I was up to something. By seven, my usual persona was concealed beneath a long, blonde wig and equally conspicuous sunglasses. The doorman turned to watch as I breezed past, though not because he recognized me. From under my navy wool coat, netted legs moved swiftly toward the elevator and I saved all eye contact for the floor.

I promised again to pick a new paint color soon and begin to rid our high-rise studio of its bachelor-pad vibe. We hadn't bothered much with furnishings and a rumpled club chair tucked alone in the corner cried desperately for my decorator's help. But this wasn't a place for swank cocktail mixers meant to cozy up with Manhattan's political elite. This was a place for fucking, pure and simple and, rightfully, the only care we'd taken was in selecting the king-size bed placed starkly in the center of the room. I dropped my coat on the arm of the chair and waited.

Mac was the first, announcing himself with the tap of his retro lighter. I invited him in, though we both knew such formalities were unnecessary; not when I could still imagine the distinct swell of his cock growing ever larger inside me. He relaxed in the chair and I returned to sit on the bed. There wasn't anything to talk about. I didn't want to know what he had planned for the weekend or if his mother had been giving him a hard time about still being single. I didn't want to hear about the interesting film he'd seen or the amazing meal he'd enjoyed or if he planned to vote for my husband. There we were, primal, basic, with no reason for meaningless chitchat. Blatantly stark, our silence was far from awkward. It was natural.

Instead, I drifted to how Jacob and I came across Mac in the first place—the sheer luck of it. An invitation to the only respectable smut fest in the city seemed too good to pass up, and the licentious disguised as curious were on their best behavior at the Met's special viewing of Victorian erotica. After a second whiskey sour, Mac casually mentioned he was a top OB/GYN at Presbyterian. A doctor that smokes is indictable enough, but a gynecologist with an affinity for forbidden pussy has a more perfect need for discretion than we could ask for.

Jingling keys outside the apartment ignited a familiar blast of adrenaline, something I still feel every time Jacob's smoldering eyes flood upon me. I sat there, excitement building, begging the lock to turn faster. He emerged a shadow among the hallway lights, slack-tied and steel jawed, focused like a maestro ready to conduct. My Jacob intended to arrange a trio of players into a complicated mélange of flesh and I would be the instrument.

He kissed me in greeting, the way a husband kisses his wife upon returning home from work, and nodded at Mac, who nodded back. Then he rubbed a bit of my Greenwich Village wig between his fingers, staring at my exaggerated kohl-lined eyes, amused for the moment with my alter ego. His gaze was interrupted by the next gaggle of knocks rapping loud and brash on the door, finding Brett standing in the hall with Lyle approaching directly behind him.

I introduced Lyle as my surprise guest, twisting my heel nervously on the floor as I waited for Jacob's response. Impetuousness, the character trait of my undoing, still seemed to tug my husband's mouth into a wily grin after all these years. He sized Lyle up; a taller image of himself, but fifteen years younger. Only Jacob was never so clean shaven during our college years, full of dirty backpacks and flap jackets. Lyle looked like he'd spent every summer on his daddy's yacht and every weekday on the trading floor downtown. I liked that about him, neat and trim just like we are now, with currents of rebellion coursing beneath the polish.

Our party complete, Jacob began to strip away my first layer.

His fingers trickled slowly around my neck, slipping into my collar and flicking my buttons loose. Designer silk fell away from my shoulders, revealing fine imported lace. Studious eyes might have questioned their departure from the rest of my cheap getup, but Lyle was more focused on the removal of these items than their cost, and I smiled toward his moistened lips, anticipating them sweeping across my skin.

Who would be first? It could have been any one of them, all delicious looking and stirring in their trousers with signs of readiness. I didn't want to decide, and thankfully, I knew I wouldn't have to. Jacob was in charge here in the id's secret little playground of vaporized regrets.

He pointed to Mac and to Lyle with a casual pass of his finger through our silence. I understood and sauntered over to Mac, topless, taking his hand and placing it on my bare chest. Then, reaching for Lyle, I offered him the same. Greedily, each of them took of me what was given, hungry with selfish urgency, splitting me in half for their share of my skin. Wet mixed with soft, tinged with dull scrapes and harsh suction. They were wild and disorganized and Jacob meant to set them straight. He stepped between them to push me gently onto the bed and part my legs. Instructions were given with as few words as necessary. This was Jacob in the raw.

"You, two fingers. And you rub her nice."

Jacob yanked my skirt up around my waist like a belt, and I stretched my netted legs wide thanks to Pilates. Mac's fingers took to examining my entrance, probing as directed, while Lyle churned my grateful clit. I reached for them both, catching collars and pulling their mouths back to duty on my breasts. There was one simple rule to follow in Jacob's playground: give me pleasure, more than I could handle. And only when I was so wet that my thighs glistened and my lips dribbled desperate pleas for release would anyone get to have me. I gritted my teeth for the decadent and agonizing ascent to the point of no return, while Jacob watched and waited.

"Though the events widely publicized in the news are greatly exaggerated, the nature of the allegation requires the withdrawal of my candidacy and my immediate resignation of this office."

I was so wet that Lyle's fingers were merely sloshing about while Mac worked me steadily inside. Still, I wasn't wet enough for Jacob's liking—not yet begging for it. I was moaning though, moaning long and loud as my hips rose and fell to Mac's rhythm, encouraging his fingers deeper. Poor Brett was stuck in Jacob's holding pattern, stroking his cock footsteps away. I wanted a

taste of it, that long sweet cock in his hand belonged in my
mouth and the thought of him pushing past my lips, heavy on
my tongue, cinched my cunt with a jolt.

I called for him, "Brett, come closer," daring Jacob to inter-
vene.

"You can't have him yet."

My voice tangled with breath on my lips. "I won't suck him,
I promise."

He nodded and Brett pressed his head against my surly pout
as I willed myself to be still, save for the tiny licks stolen from
underneath.

Brett continued to pump his hand along his shaft, oozing
salty precome over my taste buds. My pussy ignited, flooding
anew and sending me truly to the brink of my own sanity, just
like Jacob wanted.

Abruptly, my head dropped away and I made myself clear.
"Now, please Jacob, please!"

He was already sliding off his pants. "Get over here."

I took my place in his lap on that old chair and he blind-
folded me with his Hugo Boss necktie. The air smelled of sex,
dirty and pungent. I'd be sure to leave a window cracked when
we were finished, but right then I wanted to suffocate on it.
Obediently, I opened my mouth as Jacob spread me equally
agape from below. He pulled my legs roughly and danced at
my ass with slickened fingers. Ready, together, he worked his
cock into my tightest hole as another pressed toward the back
of my throat. I recognized it, the smooth shaft cast to the left
and salty-sweet like roasted almonds. Brett usually started in
my mouth.

The next cock inside me would be a mystery—and so went
the beauty of four men...musical cocks. I didn't want to know
which of them, Lyle or Mac, was stretching me to my limits,

sliding past Jacob with long definite strokes, wrapping his sweaty palm around my neck for leverage. I wanted only to imagine, to guess, to lose myself in my right of depraved ignorance—the right not to care. And I also focused on the known; the way he traded places with Jacob and staved off the urge to come in a sudden motionless protest. I sucked hard and deep on Brett, waiting for him to paint me with sticky seed, like he always did. The first molten drops came quickly as vacancy assaulted my cunt, only to be filled again before my next shower.

"Ooo—" Another cock thrust into my mouth stuffed the moan back down my throat.

Measured and controlled, Jacob kept to his own languid pace in my ass; always there, always mine. He would be the last to come, patient to the end, more concerned that I was left a shuddering ball of nerves in his arms.

"She's close. Eat her."

Whose mouth lapped roughly at my clit, bathing his chin with my silk and diving persistent fingers inside me? Whose name should I have called out when the surge swelled under my skin like an over-filled balloon?

"Oh, god, Jacob, I love you."

"I am regretful of many things, but mostly I am saddened to know that I have let all of you down. I will have to find it in myself to come to terms with that."

They had the decency to warn us at least, though the call came only moments before the big story broke on cable news. Jacob told me that they'd keep me out of it, that the report would state that he'd been at a sex party with a prostitute. I saw his mouth twitch when he said that. Jacob had never been with another woman, not even once. In an hour, I'd booked us on a flight to Ibiza scheduled to take off right after his speech.

I wonder if Lyle will do the talk-show circuit; will they drag the whole thing out until nobody even cares anymore? To hell with sticking around for that. For better or for worse, it's over. I've packed our freedom into those old backpacks I found in the hall closet behind the golf clubs. From now on, I hope it's all the baggage we'll ever need.

THE PACT

Elizabeth Coldwell

The pier was about to close for the evening by the time Catherine finally reached it. For a moment, it looked as though the fat, sullen girl in the ticket kiosk was going to refuse her admission, but in the end she relented, taking Catherine's money and pushing a thick pasteboard ticket back through the hole in the glass.

What if she were too late? Catherine wondered. What if Leon had decided she wasn't coming, that she hadn't been serious when she had arranged to see him, and had already left? She cursed her stupidity at forgetting to charge her mobile phone before she'd left North London that morning, so that by the time a signal failure had caused the train to come to an unexpected halt somewhere in the Hampshire countryside, she'd been unable to ring and let him know she was delayed.

She hurried toward the end of the pier, heels clacking on the weathered deck and coat collar turned up against the November chill. Through the gaps in the planks she could see the sea beneath her, churned up into choppy waves by the breeze. As she passed the little café halfway along the pier's length, a middle-aged woman in dowdy green overalls was already taking inside the wooden board advertising hot drinks, toasted sandwiches and ice cream, a silent declaration that no more customers were welcome. There was nothing sadder or more dispiriting than an English seaside town out of season, Catherine thought, and she wondered again why Leon had chosen to settle here. What-ever the impulse, it could be no stranger than the one that had compelled her to drop him an email a couple of days before her fortieth birthday and remind him jokingly of the pact.

The pact. How long ago it all seemed now, the night when Leon and she had first agreed to it. It wasn't a solemn moment, not as she remembered it. Indeed, it had started as a joke. But somewhere along the way, it had become a promise they repeated to each other over the years. "If neither of us is married when we're forty, then we'll marry each other."

Leon had proposed it, lying on his bed in the grim hall of residence they had found themselves in, that first year at univer-sity. They had spent the evening at a block party, drinking them-selves almost insensible on punch laden with cheap vodka. As ever, Leon had been lamenting his luck with the opposite sex.

"What is it about me, Cat?" he'd asked, arms flung out in a sacrificial pose. "Why don't they go for me?"

She knew exactly, but there was no way she could tell him without hurting him. And the reason she knew was because she felt the same. It wasn't just that Leon somehow hadn't grown into his body yet, was still gangly and awkward where other lads had gained muscle and the swagger and self-assurance that came with it. Away from home for the first time, away from the boys—and the boyfriends—they'd grown up with, the girls she knew were beginning, in their nice, Home Counties fashion, to rebel.

That meant passing over the likes of loyal, kind-hearted Leon in favor of Danny Demetriou in East Block, who had come-to-bed eyes, gel-stiff hair and the tightest jeans on campus. Her friends might have joked that the only possessions he owned were a set of dumbbells and a mirror, but they still queued up to share his bed for the fortnight or so until he tired of them and moved on to someone else. Leon was strictly best-friend material, safe and comforting, always there to help her pick up the pieces rather than cause things to fall apart in the first place.

Catherine decided not to share any of this with Leon, particularly not the details of her own, spectacularly unfulfilling three-day fling with Danny. She stared up with unfocused eyes at the Stone Roses poster he'd Blu-Tacked to the ceiling of his room. She was going to be sick as a dog in the morning, and the party hadn't even been worth the impending hangover.

"I really don't think your Aunty Cat is the best person to be giving you relationship advice," she said. "I mean, I'm just as likely to end up on my own as you are."

And those words, words she didn't actually believe at the time but which had come to seem more and more like a self-fulfilling prophecy over the years, had somehow triggered the making of the pact. They hadn't sealed it in blood, neither of them able to trust themselves near a sharp object at that moment. Instead, they had shaken hands as though completing a business deal, unable to stop themselves from giggling as they did, then Catherine had staggered back to her own room, with its too-thin mattress and random gurgling from the pipes in the block bathroom next door.

A thin, squally rain had started to fall, its cold caress bringing her sharply back to the present. There was a man slouching against the black-painted iron railing, dressed in a shabby camouflage coat and with a black woolen hat pulled down low on his brow. He straightened at her approach, and she realized it was Leon.

How long was it since she'd last seen him in the flesh? There was the party, of course, about eighteen months after they had both graduated. It had been thrown by Guy Sheen, who'd been in her History of Art tutorial group. He lived in a damp-ridden squat in Clapham and was playing at being an anarchist in the way only someone with a trust fund behind him can. That was the night Leon told her he was packing in his job and joining the army, desperate to do something that would make a difference. After that, they had only corresponded by letter and, later, email. He told her plenty about army life, the friends he'd made there, his postings to West Germany and Cyprus. Her own job, working in a small art gallery in Clerkenwell, seemed mundane and unnecessary in comparison.

When he was sent to Iraq, contact between them became more sporadic, partly because of the physical realities of his tour of duty, partly because she was in the process of separating from David, whom she'd met, married and come to realize she had absolutely nothing in common with within the space of seventeen months.

Beneath the daily grind of work and dealing with divorce lawyers, a low-level anxiety about Leon's safety nagged away at her. He sent her a photo of himself and half a dozen of the lads in his battalion, all slightly blurred, posing against a tank in Basra. She couldn't help but think how young some of them of were—the age her own sons would have been if she'd settled down after leaving school as so many of her classmates had done, rather than pursuing a university education. So young, but already showing more courage than she would ever possess.

She shivered whenever she heard on the news of British casu-

alties, offering up a silent prayer that it wouldn't be Leon who
was coming home limbless or dead. It never was, but reading
between the lines of his emails she sensed he'd come close
enough to realize he was too old for this game. At the end of
his second tour of Iraq, he wrote to tell her he was resigning his
commission and coming back to England for good.

And now he was here, smiling at her as she came nearer. He
held out his arms and invited her into a hug. "Cat, it's so good
to see you again," he murmured into her ear.

She stepped back so she could look at him properly, regis-
tering how the years had changed him. Some people thickened,
sagged and faded into themselves as they approached middle
age. Leon had matured, filling out and gaining a composure
that suited him as much as his newly steel-gray hair. The
phrase "silver fox" popped into her head from nowhere, but she
dismissed it, anxious to know how she appeared to him.

"You look fantastic," he said, eying her up and down. She
blushed at the compliment. She wasn't like some women she
knew, who exercised obsessively and lived on lettuce leaves and
fresh air, trying to retain the figure they'd had when they were
eighteen. She had thickened a little around her hips and belly,
and her breasts were so full she could no longer get away with
not wearing a bra, but she knew men—or the men who were
worth bothering about, anyway—preferred that to the half-
starved look. Leon certainly seemed to like it, from the way
he was looking at her, and she felt a sudden, unexpected flut-
tering in her pussy. It shocked her. Of all the emotions she had
expected to feel on seeing Leon again, sexual desire was not one
of them. Yet she couldn't deny something deep inside her was
responding to the innate masculinity years of army life seemed
to have honed in him.

"So why did you decide to move here?" she asked, as they

walked back down the pier toward the promenade. "Why not come back to London?"

"I used to spend all my holidays here when I was a kid," Leon replied. "It gave me a soft spot for the place. And it's quiet here. London would be too much for me now."

He didn't need to say any more. She was aware how hard it was for men to adjust to everyday life after the strict, regimented routine of the forces. Too many ended up homeless and broken, dependent on drink or drugs to get them through the day. At least Leon seemed sorted, comfortable in this new environment.

He was living in a flat five minutes' walk from the seafront, above an office supplies shop. Catherine gazed at the window display, box upon box of photocopier paper, as Leon unlocked the side door. She followed him up the stairs, waiting as he let them both inside.

Telling her to make herself at home, he went to put the kettle on. As he bustled about the tiny kitchen, she studied the room for personal touches. She was surprised to see that among the photos he had tacked up on the wall was one taken the day they had graduated. Arms around each other, they beamed into the lens, she with the curly perm that had somehow become the height of fashion in the early nineties, he with an inexpertly dyed blond fringe falling into his eyes. They looked so young, so innocent, she thought, neither of them knowing the twists and disappointments life had in store for them.

Leon wandered out with a mug in each hand and caught her studying the photo. "I can't believe I ever thought that hairstyle suited me," she said with a rueful laugh.

He handed her a mug. She took a sip, startled yet pleased to discover that even after all these years, he remembered how she liked her tea: strong but milky, the color of caramel.

As they began to talk, it was as though they were picking up exactly where they had left off, at the party in Guy Sheen's squalid flat. She brought him up to date with the gossip about the few members of their university circle with whom she was still in contact. Most of those friendships had fallen by the wayside over the years, and even with so many social networking websites available to her, she felt no temptation to try to rekindle them. The people who were important to her were still in her life—and that most definitely included Leon.

She couldn't help feeling that all the conversation, all the seizing on private jokes and completing each other's sentences, was simply leading to the moment when they ended up in bed together. It was that inevitable. Under the excuse of looking at old photographs, they were sitting so close his leg was resting tight beside hers. Neither of them had moved away when the initial contact was made, and the steady pressure of his strong, solid thigh against her own was causing her to grow increasingly wet.

Once or twice, she caught herself casting sneaky glimpses at his crotch. He was sitting in the way men so often do, legs sprawled wide to claim as much space for themselves as they can, and her eyes were drawn to where his cock bulged against his trouser zip. Twenty years ago, she would have been embarrassed to look at such a blatant display—he was her best friend, after all—but now she was anxious to see more. What did he look like when his pants came off? How big was he? Was he circumcised? Did he stick straight up when he was hard, or bend a little to one side, as David had done?

Flustered by the strength of her lust for him, she reached for her mug once more and only succeeded in spilling it down herself. Tea splashed over her sweater, staining the white wool. She pulled a tissue from her bag and began dabbing at it, apologizing for her clumsiness.

"You need to soak that, or you'll never get the mark out," he said. "Take it off, and I'll stick it in the sink."

She stared at him. He might only be thinking of the practicalities, but she couldn't start taking her clothes off in front of him, not when she'd been mentally stripping him down just moments before.

He took her silence for reticence. "Come on, Cat. Don't be shy. All those times we used to sunbathe round the back of South Block, it's not like I haven't seen you half-undressed before."

That was true, but she'd never sunned herself in anything quite like what she was wearing now, a seamless nylon bra so sheer her nipples would be clearly visible through it. Perhaps he wouldn't notice. No, that was stupid. Of course he would notice—and a small, overheated part of her so badly wanted him to.

He was holding out an impatient hand. She took a deep breath and pulled the sweater over her head. He said nothing, just dashed into the kitchen. She heard the sound of running water, then he was back.

He smiled when he saw how she was sitting, hands crossed over her chest so her breasts were covered. "Should I take my shirt off, too? Even things up a bit?"

She couldn't tell him things would only be even when they were both lying naked, bodies twined together. She wanted him so much, but she was afraid to say the words. Sex ruined friendships, everyone knew that. Perhaps that had something to do with why they'd never hooked up at university, when they'd had so many opportunities. Deep down there had always been a fear of spoiling what they already had. And yet...

Leon solved the dilemma for her, extending a hand for her to take. Helping her to her feet, he pulled her into his arms.

Even in her three-inch heels, her head still barely reached his shoulders. He bent his head, kissing her for the first time since they'd said good night on leaving Guy Sheen's party. Kissing her properly for the first time ever. Her mouth melted against his, his tongue pressing forcefully between her lips.

Where did he learn to kiss like this? she wondered as he took teasing little bites of her lower lip, then decided she didn't really care, not as long as he kept on doing it. Eyes closed, hands locked around the back of his neck, she barely registered that he was working on the catch of her bra until he had it undone and his calloused hands were cupping her bare tits. She pressed a little closer to his big body, feeling the solid bulk of his cock against her belly.

"Come on, let's take this to the bedroom," Leon suggested.

"Just a moment," she said, unzipping her skirt and shimmying out of it. She stood before him in only her flesh-colored hold-up stockings and a pair of knickers as sheer as the bra. They were so wet they clung to her shaved pussy lips, hiding nothing from him.

"Fuck me, that's nice," Leon exclaimed. "Thinking about that would have got me through a few night patrols, I can tell you."

The bedroom was barely big enough for the double bed and the wardrobe, which was all the furniture it contained. In contrast to Leon's old room in South Block, which had always had a pile of dirty laundry festering in a corner and clutter on every surface, it was almost clinically tidy, the legacy of his army days, she supposed. She lay back on the navy-striped duvet, watching as he stripped off his shirt and trousers. In his white T-shirt and dark-green shorts, he cut an impressive figure, the muscles in his chest and arms sharply defined. He'd told her he was working as a personal trainer, even though it was a waste of all his paper qualifications; she thought he looked like a pretty good advert for his own services.

He joined her on the bed and they started kissing again, Leon holding her face in his cupped palms so he could stare into her eyes. She pushed her hands up under his T-shirt, wanting to feel his firm stomach. Instead, she found her fingers running over a puckered ridge of scar tissue. He tensed for a moment, then relaxed when she didn't immediately recoil from what she could feel.

"Let me see," she murmured. He pulled the T-shirt over his head. The scar bisected his abdomen, stark white and giving the impression of being hastily stitched together. It must be a battlefield repair, she thought.

She decided against asking him how he had received such a terrible injury. She sensed there were things he had seen and done that he didn't want to talk about right now; might never want to talk about, though she wanted to be there for him when he did.

Moving down his body, she placed a tender kiss on the wounded place. From there, it was a logical progression to easing down his shorts and freeing his cock. It wasn't as long as she might have hoped, but it was thick, with a tapering head half hidden in a velvet sheath of skin. When she took hold of it, she heard his breath catch in his throat. Their eyes met.

"You can't know how long I've waited to feel you do that," he said.

"Have you waited for this, too?" she asked, and closed her lips around his cockhead. She could have done this twenty years ago, she knew. He'd been hers for the taking, but she had been too busy sharing her favors with the campus hunks. As she skillfully took him farther down her throat, she was glad she hadn't tried this earlier. In those days, she would never have had the confidence to take control, to hold his shaft in such a way that he couldn't thrust harder or deeper than felt comfortable to her. She would have done what she did with Danny Demetriou and all the other lads whose names she no longer recalled: gagged on his dick, giving pleasure and receiving none in return.

She let Leon's cock slip from her mouth, turning her attention to his balls, taut in their crinkled sac. Her fingertip skimmed the entrance to his ass, making him shudder in guilty pleasure. She would have eased her finger inside him, if she hadn't been afraid he might come the second she did.

"Let me lick you," Leon urged. "I need to know how you taste."

They swapped places, so she was lying on her back and he was crouching between her legs. At first, he didn't even remove her knickers, preferring to lick her through the already saturated fabric. It dulled the sensation just a little, making her wriggle her hips upward in search of more contact with his tongue. Just when she thought she might die if she didn't feel his mouth on her bare cunt, he ripped the knickers from her and threw the ruined garment to the floor.

The smile he flashed her was pure wickedness. "Sorry, but it's so horny to think of you going back to London with your pussy bare."

As if to reinforce his words, he took the ragged petals of her sex between his lips, sucking and nibbling on them. His hands grasped her bumcheeks, pulling her hard onto his tongue. If she thought she'd learned some tricks over the years, she couldn't quite believe the ones in Leon's arsenal. He seemed to know just where to touch her, just how long to keep her dangling over the precipice before pushing a couple of fingers up inside her, pressing at her sweet spot and sending her free-falling into orgasm.

She barely had time to catch her breath before he had rolled over and pulled her on top of him. Her lips stretched around his hefty girth, her juices trickling down his shaft to ease her path. Once he was lodged in her to the root, they took a moment to share more long, sloppy kisses. When they broke apart, pure delight shone in Leon's soft hazel eyes, as though he couldn't believe this was finally happening to him. Catherine suspected her own expression was very much the same.

Eventually, she began to move, rocking lazily on the hard length buried within her. She didn't expect to reach orgasm again—she very rarely came more than once—but as she rode Leon's cock she felt the tension building in her belly once more. He played with her tits as they fucked, pinching her nipples until bolts of sensation shot down to her core. Nothing this good could last, and almost in the same moment as Leon grunted and pumped his spunk into her in short, sharp spurts, she felt her stomach doing giddy somersaults as her pussy clenched and clenched again around his cock.

Deliciously spent, she rolled off him, resting her head on his chest as he wrapped a thick arm around her.

"I wish we'd done that years ago," Leon muttered.

No, you don't, she wanted to tell him, not really, because years ago it would have been awkward and messy and over in moments. Years ago, we wouldn't have known how to make it special for each other.

Instead, she asked, "But are you still going to hold me to the pact?"

"If you'll have me," he replied. "We always said we'd marry each other if there was no one else, and for me, there never has been anyone else. Only you, Cat, the only woman I ever wanted."

"Oh, Leon, of course I'll have you." Their lips met in a lingering kiss. If she wanted to make her train back to London, she should be leaving in the next few minutes, but life there no longer seemed to hold any attraction for her. Everything she needed, she knew now, was here in this room, and the time was finally right to make it hers.

EXPOSING
CALVIN

Rachel Kramer Bussel

L et's go to a strip club," I say, my eyes lit up. I haven't been to
one in years, and certainly never with my husband. I can see
right away from the way he looks at me that he doesn't think
we're the type of people who go to strip clubs, all that judgment
packed into one lift of his brow, a simple set of his jaw.

"Honey, what? We are not too old. We're forty-two and
forty-five? I bet there'll be guys in their seventies there!"

We're on a long weekend in New York City. The kids are
with their grandparents. I'm full of energy and excitement and
want to do something we can't, or at least, don't, do at home.
Plus I want to show him something that used to be a part of my
life. No, I was never a stripper, but I used to go to places like
that with my girlfriends, just for fun. Calvin's been once, and he
said he felt dirty about it.

"Marnie, I just don't know. I don't want to be the guy with
his tongue hanging out looking like an idiot because a woman is
taking her clothes off. I don't want them to laugh at me. Plus, I

have you," he tells me, walking toward me and pulling me close for a hug.

My Calvin is a good man, a good husband, and still hot to me. He was never drop-dead gorgeous but he is sexy in his own way, with his big, slightly balding head, his big hands, nose, body. He's six foot four and husky, whereas I'm a foot shorter and petite. Even when he's not trying to slam me against the wall, a nudge from him in that direction and I'm wet as can be. I'm usually the sexual instigator, and I don't mind. I have a higher sex drive than he does, but he's never turned me down. I've been the one to introduce toys, to get him to relax enough to let me play with his ass while I blow him, to ask him to spank me. It's not that Calvin's repressed, but there is still a part of him that thinks that other people will care what we do in bed, that feels like someone—not necessarily G-d, but someone—is watching every time we do anything the least bit risqué.

That makes me laugh because I'm not an exhibitionist, either, save for my occasional low-cut dresses, and if I thought someone was watching me get it on, I'd be self-conscious, too. We both grew up in small towns with Jewish families that were on the more buttoned-up side, but I escaped at eighteen and never looked back. Calvin, I'm afraid, is always on the verge of looking back, and in our thirteen years of marriage, my job has been to pull him forward, into both the future and the knowledge that he is an adult and can enjoy his body.

Sometimes I do things just to shake him up, like when I went on my last business trip and gave him a bottle of lube and a porn DVD that I'd originally intended to take with me. "I think she's hot," I said, pointing to Jesse Jane. I knew he'd been tempted to roll his eyes at me—the blonde with the big boobs, really?—but then I pulled him down into our easy chair and started whispering in his ear, relaying the filthiest fantasy I could think of, one that ultimately involved his cock shoved between Jesse Jane's breasts. By the time I took his cock out and started stroking it, he could barely last a minute. I know that inside him lurks the heart and soul of a pervy—a nice, friendly, pervy—guy, and I like to bring him out to play when I can.

"Let's put it this way, sweetie; I'm gonna go to a strip club and get a lap dance. You can either come with me or do whatever it is you want to do." We're staying in Times Square, and there's no lack of entertainment. We have theater tickets for Saturday night, reservations for dinner at Peter Luger's Sunday, and our days are filled with friends and art galleries and walking tours. Tonight I want to do something that is just for the two of us.

"Well, when you put it that way...I just don't want you to feel slighted if I get turned on looking at the women."

"Remember the whole porn incident? Your girlfriend Jesse Jane?" I tease him, making sure he looks me in the eyes. My sweet, sexy husband actually blushes when I say her name. "Oh, you didn't forget her?" I ask as I raise my knee and run it against his dick. I know, and, frankly, he knows, too, that I could've shacked up with my ex-boyfriend Billy, who was much more of a lout than Calvin could ever hope to be. But I didn't want Billy, I wanted Calvin, and I'm not so much trying to change him as bring out the side of him I know exists, because I've seen it, felt it, touched it. I don't want a guy who brags about how many women he's banged (for the record, I'm number three on Calvin's list, whereas my list is considerably longer) or ogles every woman he comes across. This isn't so much about the women in the club, as sharing the aura of a strip club with the man I love. And for the record, I wouldn't have really gone there by myself; where's the fun in that?

"But you can't wear that," I tell him, pointing at his overly fussy shirt and dress pants. It's basically a suit without the jacket. "Put on something more casual."

I strip off my jeans and T-shirt and start rummaging through my suitcase, and while I'm bent over, my thong-clad butt in the air, Calvin comes over and takes a little nip with his teeth. Then his mouth shifts, and he's tonguing my pussy through my underwear. He slides them aside and I somehow reach for a little clingy black dress while he goes down on me. I don't say a word because I don't want to break the spell, but soon my thong is around my knees and my husband is kneeling on the floor going to town. He is so good at getting me off like this, and I know that he'd happily stay here all night. I rub against him, press myself down, take everything he's offering. His tongue plunges inside me, pressing upward, then toward the back, before moving on to my clit, but he makes sure to add two fingers. I've taken up to four of his fingers, but two is the magic number. The combination of his fingers and mouth make me go wild, and I clutch the wall with my right hand for support as my pussy tightens, bearing down on him as he finds my G-spot along with the most sensitive part of my clit. He twists and presses his fingers deep inside me while his tongue works its magic and soon I'm shuddering, stamping my foot on the ground, coming hard.

Only when he's ridden out my orgasm with me does he ease the thong off of me then gently pick out another thong and help me step into it followed by an orange silk wrap dress I love because it feels like it's stroking me all over and makes me know I won't fade away against the myriad of beautiful women we're about to see. Calvin likes the dress because it's so light, it's easy to lift it up, or undo the sash holding it together, and get to whatever part of me he's most hungry for. He stands up and doesn't say anything but I can see on his face that the unexpected bliss we just shared was just as powerful for him as it was for me. Calvin's the kind of guy who lives for giving head;

any time I want him to do something around the house, all I have to do is promise him my pussy to feast on and he moves immediately into action.

I'm quiet as I finish getting dressed, adding earrings, a little mascara, black eyeliner, and gloss. It's a tricky thing, getting dressed to go to a strip club. You don't want to look like you're trying too hard, like you want to outshine the true stars of the evening. Calvin is quiet, too, and I'm not sure if I've pushed him too far, but I hope not. I am wet at the thought of seeing him surrounded by beautiful women. I don't know why, exactly, especially when many wives would be up in arms at the prospect of their husbands even setting foot in such a place. But I'm cut from a different, naughtier kind of cloth. I think the prospect of seeing a gorgeous woman—glittering, preening, perfect, really—giving her all to making my husband hard, horny and happy, is the perfect way to spend an evening in the Big Apple.

We set out the door, holding hands in the elevator. I overhear another couple talking about the fancy dinner they're about to share and stare at the man, wondering if he'd rather be joining us on our little naked adventure. I've done a little research and found a club that doesn't serve alcohol, which means the women are totally nude. I would've been happy with sexy G-strings but I want to give my man a real treat, want to see him struggle between the side of him that thinks this is somehow improper and the side that would love nothing more than to take a trip to the champagne room with a woman who's built for sex, or at least, is selling us on that image.

We walk to the club, and I smile at the man checking us in as I give him our IDs. He leads us to two chairs that have a view of the stage, but are separated from the other patrons a little. Almost immediately, a svelte woman with black bangs and hair that slithers down her back greets us. "Hello," she says, beaming at both of us. "Can I get you a drink, or perhaps a bottle?" I've set aside cash for tonight, because I don't want that to be an issue.

"A bottle of Veuve Clicquot," I say, and she smiles and walks away briskly.

"You planned this?" Calvin asks, looking a little stunned.

"Maybe," I tell him. "Why, do you have an objection? Is it a hardship to be surrounded by so many hot women?"

"No, not at all." I can tell he wants to tack on something more, but I put my finger to his lips.

"So then enjoy it. I plan to." With that, I tug him down into his seat. He just stares at me, then at the woman who approaches us. She's short and petite, the opposite of my five nine and major curves. I can tell immediately that he likes her.

"Hello," I say to her. "I think my husband would like a dance. This is Calvin, and I'm Marnie."

The girl giggles, then says, "I'm Aurora, and I'd love to give you a dance. Is it for both of you?"

Calvin is about to nod when I shake my head. "I want him to get the dance, but I'll watch. Maybe I'll get my own after. I don't really like to share," I say, letting my eyes do the talking.

She winks at me, then walks over and whispers something into Calvin's ear before rumpling his hair. She takes off his glasses and even before the next song is officially on, she is starting to put the moves on my man. His head is thrust into her cleavage and I turn just enough to fully absorb what's happening. I see him slowly start to surrender—to her, and to me, to the idea that it's okay to want her, okay to get hard, okay to succumb to the beauty all around us. And it is beauty, even though I know so much of it is artifice. I don't mind, because I can separate the two, and focus on just the former.

I can admire Aurora's ass covered in just a glinting gold

thong, her feet raised on five-inch black and gold shoes, her nipples so perky as she rubs them right up against my husband's cheek. I have a feeling she probably wouldn't be quite so touchy if I wasn't here, but maybe she really does like him, or just wants a good tip. I don't really care, because the sight is making me want to touch myself. When the song officially starts and she bends over, thrusting her tits out to the club while her round ass, small yet firm, backs up against my husband, I put my index finger in my mouth, bent at the knuckle, needing somewhere for my oral fixation to land.

Suddenly I almost wish we'd hired a woman who'd do more than Aurora would, because I'm aching to suck her nipples, and to have Calvin know I'm sucking her nipples. He looks over at me and seeing me with my finger in my mouth makes him shudder. Then a new fantasy washes over me: I want to be the one giving Calvin a lap dance, right here, right now. I want the eyes of envious men staring over at us; strip clubs seem to be the land of the grass always being greener.

I like that aspect of what we're doing as much as anything; I want people to know we're together, to know that I'm not just putting up with my husband getting a sexy dance from a crazy-hot chick, but that I'm loving every minute, that I'm paying for it. I reach for his hand and when our fingers touch, the spark is electric. I smile at him and he seems to let out a silent groan, almost overcome with delight at what Aurora is doing.

The song can't be more than four minutes long, but it seems to last for ten. When she's done, she whispers something else to him, kisses his cheek then comes over to me. I hand her her fee, then slip an extra twenty down her G-string. "He's a lucky man," she whispers in my ear, filling me with her sweet, special scent. She stays poised at my ear for a few seconds longer than she needs to, and it's my turn to shudder. Truth be told, I'd love to feel her rub her body up against me, but not here, not now, not with all the men ready to circle like vultures, to turn something admittedly wanton but also a little bit sensual into mere masturbation fodder. Plus I want, more than anything, to talk to Calvin, to hear from him exactly what it was like.

"Next time," I whisper in her ear and I'm treated to a kiss on my cheek, too, and a brush of my lips across her breasts, a whisper of what I'm giving up. Yes, I know she works on tips, but there is something unmistakable about the way this woman moves, and either she's the best actress in the world or she's as bisexual as I am, the kind of woman who tends to go for guys until a woman comes along and makes her head spin.

She smiles and, holding hands again, Calvin and I watch her sashay across the room. The look on his face when I turn to him reminds me of when he wakes up from a wet dream, like he can't quite believe what's just happened and wishes, at least a little, it were still happening. "Are you ready to go?" I ask him.

"We can go to a club back home, too, sometime."

He just looks at me for a moment, then stands, pulls me up and gives me one of the most passionate kisses we've ever shared. This is big, for him: to grab my ass and shove his tongue in my mouth and press his hips right up against mine in public like that. I love knowing that people are looking at us, that they see how much we want each other. As we walk out, I let my curiosity bubble over. "What did she whisper to you?"

"How badly do you want to know?" Calvin asks, and it's my turn to swat his ass.

"Just tell me! This was my idea, I think I deserve to know."

"Okay, okay, don't get bent out of shape. Or do..." he says suggestively, moving to bend me as much as he can while we're out on the street. "She said that she hopes I lick your pussy really good tonight, that she hopes I show you a good time in exchange for buying me the dance. Actually, she made me promise I'd lick your pussy until you came."

"I wonder if she's thinking about you with your head between my legs right now," I whisper in his ear as we waited for a light. "I hope so. I think that'd be hot. I think it'd be hot if she watched us, if she were right there in the room while you licked me."

My normally mild-mannered husband then pulls me aside, away from the corner, and backs me up against a brick wall. His hand goes to my ass and starts massaging it, and I can feel his hardness pressing against me. "Tell me more, Marnie. Tell me what you want Aurora to do." Then he somehow positions his body so he's blocking me from view of the busiest street we're near and slides his hand along the slit of the silk dress, then up, up, up, until he's at my panties. Anyone walking by on the other side would probably notice something odd, but I don't mind. I'm thinking about Aurora, about her pressing her ass against him, about her whispering in his ear.

"I'd want her to suck your cock while I lick her pussy," I say, suddenly grateful for the cool air, for the fact that I can close my eyes and hear all the city sounds roaring around me and not think quite as much about how that idea makes me blush, makes me shake, makes me—who thought I was so sophisticated and blasé about strippers—tingle as his fingers slide inside me. The power has shifted from me to him, and Calvin knows it as he works his digits deep into me, pressing softly but in exactly the right spot, his thumb caressing my clit.

"I can hear her sucking you, swallowing you, and feel how wet it's making her. I love knowing she's getting so turned on by your big dick." I have to stop talking because what he's doing to me is just too much. Well, not so much that I want him to stop, but too much to enjoy while I'm talking. Calvin's lips swoop in to kiss me while he fucks me harder. I think he might be trying to say something into my mouth but I'm not really sure, I just know that I feel Aurora's spirit here with us as Calvin makes me come with his fingers, trapping me against the wall so I don't fall down.

Finally, he's done, and he pulls his hand out and lets my dress fall back down while I rush to retie it. "You were right, Marn. We're not too old at all. Now come on, don't dawdle. I have a promise to Aurora to keep."

When we get to the hotel, Calvin strips me naked and positions me so my ass is flush with the window, which faces another hotel's windows and is probably visible from several office buildings. There he gets down on his knees and eats me to three more orgasms, only letting me taste my fill of him when I assure him that I'm more than satisfied, for the moment, anyway.

It turns out exposure goes both ways, and I'm more than ready to bare myself to millions of strangers if it means discovering a new side to the man I thought I knew better than anyone. I may have to go back and thank Aurora before we leave. I think she deserves to know that Calvin is very much a man of his word.

SIX EYES, TWO EARS

Kris Adams

Xolani paced outside the communal house, the sound of the festivities growing weak with the fading light. Her wrap dress dug into her chest, and her flowery headdress felt more cumbersome than usual. For all the care she'd taken to look her best—young, vibrant and fertile—no one noticed her, Babatunde's *first* wife. The entire village's attention was focused on young Amara, with her smooth skin, bright eyes, and child-bearing hips. It was Babatunde's hope that he would produce a son and heir on his second wedding night. His first wife had no choice but to stand by, watch and listen.

Over the years, Xolani had learned to turn a blind eye to her husband's indiscretions with unmarried women, lonely widows, or random servants eager to please the wealthiest man in the village. The hunger he felt for them had nothing to do with her, Xolani always told herself. A new wife, though, was a direct reflection on her. After five years and no children, Babatunde was finally replacing her. Shame wrapped around Xolani's body like a thick serpent, intent on squeezing out her remaining dignity. Disgusted, Xolani trudged through the tall grass and dirt to the mud-brick house she would now have to share with another woman.

The giggling was the worst. Xolani hadn't heard giggling like that since she herself was a new bride, when her husband was still excited by her. At least Babatunde's lovers had the decency to be quiet. Amara was sounding every bit the young woman she was as she shook and shimmied for her new husband. Xolani watched silently from a stool outside the east side window. There was no curtain; if the newlyweds bothered to look, they would see Xolani there, watching them as she removed her headwrap, letting loose a mass of thin, red-dyed dreads. She remembered how Babatunde had once enjoyed taking her from behind, grabbing her thick locks in his hands as he pounded into her. Now he seemed more taken with Amara's short-cropped hair. He rubbed his hands over her finely shaped head, pressing her suggestively down to her knees in front of him.

"Husband!" giggled the new bride, "do you want me to stain my wedding boubou?"

"Not at all. Come here, girl." The two wives were not so terribly different in age, yet Xolani felt old as she watched Amara coquettishly lift her white kaftan over her head. Their husband clucked appreciatively at the girl, wasting no time in peeling the thin underclothes from Amara's skin. The giggles continued, but became softer, sulkier. This was no virgin, as Xolani had been on her wedding night. Amara swayed her wide hips with practiced ease as she stepped between Babatunde's knees, pressing his balding head between her breasts. His hands sweeping up and down her back seemed to Xolani to know their path already. Babatunde had not simply picked this girl— they were already lovers. Xolani cursed under her breath. She squeezed her eyes shut, but she could still recall Babatunde's hands on the small of Amara's back, her foot sliding lazily up and down his calf, his hands kneading her full, sweet bottom.

"You like what you see?" asked the new bride as she pressed her knee against the front of her husband's kaftan suit. "I see that you do," she growled, squeaking when Babatunde pulled her down into his lap. Xolani knew that squeal; it was the same for her when he grabbed her, wanted her, needed her, no matter the time of day. It bothered Xolani that she still needed this man so much, when he obviously did not feel the same. Could his desires be so great that one wife could not meet them? Was the need of an heir truly more enticing than the gifts she'd been bestowing upon him for nearly five years? How many nights had she lain awake while he disappeared to one of his dalliances, leaving her to find ways to quiet the longing within her alone? Before, he always came back to her. Now, he would have no need.

Once she'd had enough, Xolani wiped angry tears from her cheeks, and prepared to take one last look. She'd seen her co-wife around a few times, always dressed in the richest, most flattering fabrics. Never before had she seen the young woman completely naked. Her mahogany skin glowed against the flickering light of the oil lamps illuminating the house. She lay back on the low bed, long arms and legs at all angles, not at all shy of her new husband's gaze. Xolani wanted to cry again; she'd never been so carefree.

Babatunde's hands looked large and clunky as he explored his new wife. Xolani watched through tears as her husband fondled Amara's breasts. Xolani's skin itched as she watched her husband's greedy tongue search out Amara's nipples, large and dark and perfect for nursing.

"Enough...stop this." Xolani wasn't sure to whom she was

whispering. No one was forcing her to witness this consummation, yet she continued, despite the ache developing in her head, her eyes, her belly. Best to know the enemy, she told herself. Only then could she outsmart, outlove her co-wife. "Yes," she told herself, her gods, her ancestors, "that is the only way."

Wiping away the last tears, Xolani leaned closer, resting her head and arms on the damp windowsill, a reluctant yet attentive student. She observed how Amara stretched and arched her back, pushing her breasts into her husband's waiting mouth, feeding him her erect nipples. Amara ordered Babatunde to rid himself of his pants, lest she do it for him. Xolani told herself she would have to be demanding as well, especially if such forthrightness elicited such an emphatic response from their shared husband. Shimmying out of his clothes, Babatunde grasped the thickness between his legs and spread his wife's thighs. Xolani ducked to get a better look. The hair between Amara's legs was sparse, her outer labia full and dark, and her *kuma* seemed to open and glisten when Babatunde teased it with his cock. Amara purred happily, slid a hand down to stroke at her inner lips, the hood of her clitoris, but her husband pushed her hand away before she could penetrate herself, like Xolani wanted her to, she was disgusted to realize.

With no additional preparation, Babatunde pulled Amara to him, his cock filling her with ease. He pressed down on top of her, riding her with all the speed and strength that Xolani recognized from their own lovemaking. She wondered, in her anger, if Amara was enjoying this, being pounded into the bed with little regard for what looked like quite an erection of her own. Xolani crossed her legs, not wanting to think too hard upon Amara's sex, or her full breasts, or her wetness sticking to their husband's swollen cock. They made such noise—Babatunde's huffing and puffing, Amara's high moans—

that Xolani wondered if the whole village could hear them.

When she heard footsteps nearby, she was sure she was right, that the elders had come to stop this overindulgence. But it was only Jomo, Babatunde's favorite servant and near-constant companion. When he approached the house, Xolani hissed at him, and he skulked away, head lowered, into the night. The triumph was momentary; Xolani bit back a curse at the newly-weds' changing position. With Amara on top, Xolani could better see her tiny back arching, his hands squeezing her ass, her vagina swallowing his dark shaft, all the time with Amara squealing and moaning like an animal.

Xolani wondered as she toyed absentmindedly with her nipples poking through her kaftan, *is this what Babatunde likes?* His climax, full of noise and vigor and squeezing of breasts, was answer enough. Xolani pressed her nails into her palms, punishment for watching, for not running away, for wanting to see more. And for the dampness she could not ignore between her legs. She watched them part and fall onto their backs, wife catching her breath, husband quickly falling to sleep. For all her previous vocalization, Amara appeared unfulfilled, and quite used to it. Xolani couldn't quite bring herself to feel sorry for her co-wife, but she understood.

Xolani rushed to her small private house as quietly as she could and threw herself on her bed. Only after she'd ripped her kaftan off and masturbated through tears could she finally fall asleep.

The night was crisp, almost cold, but Amara left her warm shawl behind as she ventured out into the wilderness. It had been nearly two weeks since her husband left her on business, and her skin was feeling its neglect. She'd become accustomed to his constant attentions in their short marriage, and even though he was nearly twice her age, she looked forward to his affections, perhaps more than she'd expected. So she decided to surprise Babatunde on his return home, and perhaps enjoy some time alone with him near the cool river, away from the constant prying eyes of the servants, the other villagers and his other wife.

The more she thought about how happy Babatunde would be when he found her, the more excited Amara became. She covered her mouth, holding back the girlish giggles that might give away the surprise. He would be off the path, closer to the river, with his new purchase of livestock. His growing wealth made him even more attractive to her...and to other women in their tribe. Amara knew it was too early for her to worry about competition. It was enough that her husband still wanted her...when he wasn't otherwise occupied.

Once enough stars lit the sky, Amara could see far enough down the river to discern a campfire. Closer, and she could hear and smell the cattle. At fifty cubits from the fire, she finally found her husband lounging on the ground atop a makeshift bed of straw and branches. Smiling hopefully, she crouched down and crept silently through the tall grass, waiting for the perfect moment to make her presence known and initiate their reunion.

She didn't think anything of it when Jomo appeared out of the darkness, naked from the waist up. Babatunde's pet followed the man practically everywhere. Amara sometimes teased her husband that the young man hoped that by ingratiating himself to his master over the years, he would earn a large reward upon Babatunde's death, or better yet, be released from his servitude early. Her husband always laughed at her then shut her up with his mouth, or his firm hand on her bottom. Amara watched the young man strip down to his undergarment and still thought it only slightly odd. Why would Babatunde allow his servant to share his bed, no matter how crude, no matter how remote? She crept closer, never taking her eyes off the young man's strong chest and arms. Crouching down behind a large rock, she stared and waited, her heart thumping in her chest. The big cats had nothing on her.

"The night air chills," she heard her husband say. With outstretched arms, he smiled like one of the kings of old, awaiting tribute from faithful servants. "Warm me, Jomo." It angered Amara that her husband would use on this minion words he so often used on her, when he beckoned her to his bed instead of Xolani. She was already smarting from that when Jomo slipped quickly out of his garments and flopped down on top of her husband into a long, silent kiss.

"Has the boy gone mad?" Amara whispered to herself, as if by speaking the words, that would make it true, and explain why her husband was, right before her eyes, kissing and stroking this young peon. That it was a man, a servant, or anyone besides his first wife: she did not know which of these hurt more. She'd heard whispers about men who'd take as lovers males on the cusp of manhood; one seeking renewed youth, the other seeking a mentor, or protection. It never occurred to Amara that her husband held such predilections, yet he appeared quite comfortable and practiced in the art of love with a man. Her knees digging into the hard earth, she watched with a mixture of fascination and abhorrence as Babatunde stretched the youth out before him, running his pale palms over Jomo's chestnut skin. It frightened her to watch, and it frightened her not to watch. What would happen if she stopped watching?

"Your beauty has not faded," Babatunde cooed as he lifted the boy's limbs one by one to inspect in the firelight. "Not yet... not yet." Amara fumed; shock aside, it maddened her to think that her husband would scrutinize her the same way, looking for signs of aging even when she was still so young. She hated Jomo, but a part of her felt sorry for him, the way his eyes stayed constant on her husband, the way his body was compliant for Babatunde's every touch. She recognized that look on the boy's face—he was in love, and Babatunde probably didn't notice or care. Amara shook her head, squeezed her eyes shut and slapped the ground with her small hands, as if it would do any good.

"Did you hear something, sir?"

"I hear nothing but the river," Babatunde replied, calming his young lover with a rough kiss. Amara wanted to crawl away home. She wanted to run to them, kicking and screaming and cursing their ancestors. She wanted to die. What she didn't want was to keep watching, but somehow she couldn't look away. So she sat back and watched through her fingers, grudgingly fascinated at the way her husband looked grinding his body against this young man. It was so odd: the long, strong legs that wrapped around her husband's hips. She cried silently, not just for herself, but, uncannily, for Xolani as well.

She was already rocking back and forth, dismayed and captivated, when her husband suddenly jumped to his feet and snatched off his undergarment. His *mboo* was long and full, and Amara wondered just what he planned to do with it. Her breath caught when Jomo, ever eager, crawled to his knees and gratefully accepted Babatunde's penis into his mouth. She could barely keep herself from crying aloud; this was an act considered almost taboo to her people. The elders warned that such things were dirty, only to be attempted when a man was too infirm for sex, or his wife too heavy with child. The younger generation was less likely to conform to such traditions, and Amara had several times offered to love her husband this way. He would always brush her away without explanation, only to then flip her over and slide his angry cock into her. She would then soon forget the offer. But she wouldn't soon forget this, how Babatunde breathed deep and loud as Jomo sucked him, how he pulled on the boy's thick curls as he pulsed his hips, driving his penis farther. Amara stared with rapt fascination as Jomo pressed back the foreskin and lapped at the head of her husband's penis. Babatunde grumbled his approval, deep and gravelly, like Amara had never heard. She'd never seen her husband grow so hard so fast. It shamed her, it pained her and it excited her. Always had her husband's erection come from her hand, the friction against her belly or thigh, or from the slick lips of her *kuma*. If she had known how much Babatunde enjoyed this, maybe she would have insisted on being given the chance to try again. Could it be that it looked like...fun?

"Nothing feels as good as the warmth of your mouth," Babatunde growled, smiling as he rubbed his testicles. Amara could just make out a subtle smile around the corners of Jomo's mouth. She leaned closer to get a better look, and yes, he was smiling as well as he could, with her husband's thickness sliding long and slow down his throat. Amara wondered what it tasted like, if it was anything like her fingers after she was forced to give herself pleasure because her husband was sharing his other wife's bed. Now she realized that he was most likely with Jomo on those cold nights.

When Babatunde shoved the boy away, Amara hoped the torment would cease, that he would take his *mboo* in hand and bring himself off right there, and be done with it. Her hope was dashed, her unease continued, when her husband clucked his tongue, and Jomo, as if by rote, flopped onto the makeshift bed on his belly, his ass perched high, waiting. Amara gasped. If they heard her, they did not stop. She recognized the look in her husband's eyes well enough to know his intention. Wetting his palm with saliva, Babatunde kneeled behind the young man as he stroked his glistening cock.

"Did you bring the oil?" he asked, his voice shaky with desire. "Did you?"

Jomo looked nervous. "I am sorry, sir. I've forgotten."

"So pretty, and yet so forgetful." Babatunde shimmied up against Jomo's raised backside and slid his wet cock into the cleft of the boy's buttocks. "Shall I take you anyway?" Jomo, now breathing fast and anxious, looked over his shoulder.

"If that is your desire, sir."

"My desire." Babatunde laughed heartily, thrusting with more vigor against the young man's body. "I suspect that would be *your* desire, my young friend. Since you disappoint me with your ineptitude, I think that tonight I will not give in." Jomo squirmed like a spoilt child, but Babatunde merely clucked his tongue. "No. I shall not fuck you tonight."

Amara's mouth went dry. Her husband...Jomo...*that*. She watched in a daze as Babatunde thrust his cock between Jomo's tightly squeezed thighs. The boy gasped, from relief or disappointment, she was not sure. As she watched her husband ride Jomo faster, spearing his thighs as he kissed and bit the skin underneath him, Amara was unsure whether she was disappointed or relieved. That Babatunde would...could...make love to this boy was never in her conception. They had obviously done it before, and they would do it again. She asked herself: Could she live with this? Could she stand for this?

Could she stand to look away?

She was not surprised when her husband's grunts and thrusts sped up, and he called out into the night his impending release. Jomo moved along with him, whispered to him, encouraged him, but his own cock lay neglected against the branches of their bed. Amara managed a bit of pity for the young man.

Babatunde could never be accused of being generous in the act of love, even with her. It was something she'd always hoped for, that he would reciprocate with his hands or mouth after he found his own pleasure. More often than not, Babatunde would fall asleep on top of her, leaving her unsated and sticky. She couldn't help wondering...what will Jomo do afterward?

He was louder than she expected when he came, thrusting like a wild horse between his servant's thighs, crowing like a rooster to the sky. For his part, Jomo did not ask for anything, nor did he push Babatunde off of him when the man fell atop him, exhausted and happy. She cursed him as much as she pitied him—was that what Babatunde wanted? Did he resent her repeated begging for her own pleasure? Could anyone, even a servant, live so unsatisfied and unappreciated?

Amara's new tears were a surprise. She wiped them, looked at them, wondered for whom they were shed.

The stars did not follow her home, and in the darkness and the blindness of tears, Amara stumbled into her co-wife sleeping in the master bed.

"What do you want?" Xolani hissed. "Isn't it your night with our husband?"

"I thought it was," Amara replied ruefully. "I went out to surprise him, for I have great news, but...apparently, he makes his bed with Jomo tonight."

Xolani curled into a tight ball under her covers. "I know. Get used to it."

Jomo walked awkwardly through the village, an erection brought on by his master's affections left to scratch uncomfortably against his sticky clothing. If he had any time to himself, he would disappear into the night, spill his seed to the earth and find a few hours peace before work began anew at sunrise.

But Babatunde had one last command before he fell asleep, and Jomo rushed to have it realized.

Normally it would only take a moment for Jomo to place the wild herbs atop Amara's doorstep. The elders told Babatunde that this was a surefire way to ensure the baby his second wife was carrying would be male. Since Amara started showing, Jomo had spent nearly half his day collecting the plants. On this night, though, the swelling in his sex was too great, and he had to stop momentarily to catch his breath. When he happened to look up, he caught a glimpse through the open door of Amara preparing to bathe. Jomo quickly looked away; he could be soundly punished for such an invasion. But the night was still, and Babatunde was out cold in the communal house. Jomo dared to look back, and was shocked to find his mistress naked. Her belly was full and solid, and she still had several months to go. Her breasts had filled out, along with her thighs and back-side, and she looked at once like sculpted images of fertility goddesses. He smiled sadly at her beauty.

He hadn't noticed Xolani until she came forward with a basin and soapy cloth to wash Amara's back. He shrank back, as he was admittedly a little afraid of the first wife. She had yet to warm to him, as Amara had done, slowly, ever since she became pregnant. He watched Xolani scrub the younger wife's skin, roughly at first, a look of disgust on her face. That it would pain Xolani to be confronted with her own wifely failures at such close range pleased Jomo. He watched Xolani wash the small of the back, the full bottom, the backs of the thighs, the calves. Amara simply closed her eyes. There was serenity about the scene that belied the brewing anger in Xolani's face, or the still-stirring prominence in Jomo's pants.

Once finished, Xolani doused Amara with heated water from a pitcher, rinsing the back of her body before quietly uttering,

"Turn around." Amara was not shy in front of her co-wife; she stood straight, arms extended, chest high. Xolani paused, looking a little embarrassed when she moved to the full breasts, taking more care around the enlarged nipples and the distended belly. On her knees, Xolani lifted Amara's leg on a stool and tended to the thighs, the calves, then back up to the dark curls between the legs. Blushing, Xolani washed the genitals quickly but tenderly. When she turned for the pitcher, she wiped her eyes.

Xolani was on her knees, drying her co-wife's feet with a large sheet, when Amara cleared her throat and asked, "Shall we bathe you now?" Before Xolani could answer, Amara had her on her feet and was clumsily undoing her wrap dress. "As large as I am, our husband will not likely lay with me any time soon. He may come to you tonight, so you should be ready."

Xolani's eyes were wide, but she did not stop Amara from undressing her. "I suspect he'll be with his favorite pet. We may not see him until your son is born."

"Perhaps," Amara said. "Later than that, if it is a girl."

"If this is a girl," Xolani chuckled as she laid her hands on Amara's bare belly, "the next time we see Babatunde, he'll be bringing us a new wife!"

Jomo sat back and watched the women laugh, and part of him wanted to join them. He knew, if they didn't, that Xolani was probably right. Their husband had enough wealth for several wives, and enough sexual appetite for lovers in addition. Jomo told himself that Babatunde would have no other men, but it was only a dream. Soon Babatunde would tire of him, and seek out younger men to educate, protect and initiate into manhood. Jomo could see it as clear as the belly before his eyes.

He wondered, as the giggling women set about bathing the first wife, if he would ever have children of his own, wives to provide for and beautiful young men to satisfy his every need.

Only Babatunde could decide when their time together would cease, and Jomo longed for it as much as he dreaded it. He worried that the arrival of children would only create more work for him, in Babatunde's house and in his bed. More than that, he worried that their husband would forget about him altogether. And for a moment, Jomo wondered what life for him would be if Xolani and Amara were to disappear. Such thoughts disgusted him to tears.

Amara remained naked as she rinsed Xolani's back. They giggled at some joke, but didn't say much as Xolani tended to her own neck and chest. Suddenly Amara grabbed her from behind, one hand on her co-wife's breast, the other on her flat belly.

"It's been so long since I've felt my own body," Amara explained sheepishly.

Xolani turned around, allowing Amara to gently fondle the smaller, perkier breasts before reaching hesitantly to Amara's full, heavy breasts. "If I had been blessed by the gods to have children, I suppose this would be what I would look like," she whispered as she rolled the nipples between her fingers. Amara exhaled slowly, and arched her back. Xolani smiled and leaned down to bury her face between Amara's breasts before kissing them one after the other. She quickly lowered to her knees in the damp earth floor and slowly sucked a hardened nipple into her mouth. Whatever animosity the wives held for each other seemed to disappear, like Xolani's hands disappearing beneath Amara's belly. The second wife made a purring noise and threw her head back.

Jomo wanted to cover his eyes, because it had been so long since he'd been with anyone other than Babatunde, and because he'd never looked at a pregnant woman in such a way, and because he still couldn't help resenting these women, their future

babies, and their place in their husband's life. But he couldn't
help it, not with Xolani leading her co-wife to the bed, not
when they kissed slowly, more patiently than Babatunde ever
would, and not when Amara lay back to invite Xolani to her
glistening pudenda. Jomo knew his master disliked the taste of
woman; he'd told him as much several times. Xolani appeared
to enjoy it, as did Amara when she asked for her turn. The
women giggled like naughty schoolgirls as they switched places
and positions, to Jomo's torment. He'd already been subtly
stroking his cock through his pants when Amara reached into
a nearby basket for a phallus-shaped wood-carved dildo. With
this inside her vagina, and her co-wife's lips and fingers on her
clitoris, Amara climaxed into a fit of loud, triumphant giggles.
Jomo pulled his cock free and began stroking fast, watching
intently the way Amara reciprocated on Xolani with a slightly
bent zucchini. The first wife was less vocal, but her climax was
no less intense, and her moans of pleasure sounded like cries as
Amara finished lapping at her sex. Jomo wondered what they
would do next, wondered what they would do after, wondered
if they would mind him watching. And then he heard Babatunde calling for him.

It was an easy decision; Jomo raced away from his master's
voice, and found a bed of his own, under the stars, away from
chores and duty and frustration, and stroked himself to release,
all on his own.

The roar of the children, the villagers, and the chanting medicine men soon fell away, leaving Babatunde to linger on his
deathbed. Age had come upon him before he was ready, and
all but his first two wives had left the house, chasing after their
own children, their own younger lovers. Whatever sickness had
robbed him of his sight and strength had left his hearing nearly

intact, so he could clearly discern Xolani and Amara on the other side of the large communal house, whispering to each other. Soon they were joined by a male voice he didn't at first recognize.

Only when his wives cried to the man, kissed him and called him Jomo did Babatunde finally understand what he'd missed. Little more than an arm's reach away, the three comforted each other with their kisses and bodies. Did they think him already dead, he wondered, as Jomo complimented Amara on her ability to suck his cock, as Xolani described how delicious her co-wife's sex tasted, as both argued over who would fuck Jomo first? There Babatunde lay, filled with regret at all the four of them could have shared, if he'd not been so selfish with his love. Had he ever told any of them, or his other wives and lovers, that he loved them? He was too sick to tell them now, and they were too involved with each other, cheating him out of his rightfully earned and owned pleasure. He wished he could hate them, but the sounds coming from his lovers left his heart light as he began to fade. Babatunde wondered if ever before a man had died with both tears in his eyes and an erection in his pants, as the ancestors came for him.

RENEWAL

Delilah Night

I stood in the mall restroom looking into a mirror—at a stranger. I'd been wearing this tank top for three days. My hair looked dull. I surreptitiously took a whiff and winced. My shorts, once sassily tight on my curvy ass, were hanging onto my hips by a prayer. Two bouts of pregnancy in two and a half years, each comprised of nine months of puking, had left me thinner than I'd ever been.

Immediately I dialed my closest friend in Singapore. "Jen, why didn't you tell me I looked like hell? I thought you were my friend."

"You look like the mom of two kids under the age of three. Which you are. You have enough to deal with without me critiquing your fashion choices. And besides, you've lost so much weight—I think you're looking great! Cara, buy yourself a new dress, ask your helper to watch the kids a bit longer and get a pedicure. You totally deserve it! But don't beat yourself up for looking like a mom. You *are* a mom. Speaking of which—

NATHANIEL ADDISON MASSI, PUT THAT DOWN NOW! Gotta go." The line went dead.

I looked back at the woman in the mirror. She didn't look like the kind of woman who'd greeted her man with a plastic tarp, frosting and sprinkles on his birthday and then invited him to decorate her as his ideal birthday cake and eat her. She looked like the kind of woman who would yell at kids for spilling sprinkles on the floor as she pushed a gigantic bra strap back into place.

I frowned. When did I start wearing...? Right, nursing bras.

Well, my life and my marriage might be shit, but I didn't have to look like it. First things first: Adam had been weaned for over a month now. Not even bothering to step into a stall, I reached back and undid the monstrous clasps. Liberating my breasts from their polyester prison brought a grin to the stranger's face in the mirror. As I left the bathroom, I thrust the nursing bra into the trash.

Justin and I met in college. He was a business major with a laser focus on landing a job on Wall Street. I was a dreamy history major more interested in learning about the history of women and sex than in any practical application of that knowledge post-graduation.

At first glance, we looked totally wrong for each other. He was tall and fit. His thick brown hair was ruthlessly groomed. Even as an undergraduate, Justin was rarely seen without a tie. I was short, and my body showed my preference for books over the gym. I wasn't fat, but I would never be referred to as "svelte." I had messy red hair too often kept in place by a pencil for lack of anything else on hand. I owned nothing that needed dry cleaning. And I had long since eschewed bras as too constrictive on my C-cups (it wasn't like they were DDs, I'd once told my mother in exasperation).

There was something magnetic that kept pulling us together; that shared fondness for Mel Brooks movies bordering on the obsessive, the way we'd talk on long drives to nowhere in particular, the way we scraped money together all semester to travel all summer…and the sex.

Justin's buttoned-up exterior, as it turned out, was the iron suit worn by a man raised in a family whose motto was "What will the neighbors/members of our synagogue think?" He hadn't been allowed to get too dirty or come home too late. It was unacceptable to have a less than stellar report card. If he did an extracurricular activity, he'd better become the president/star/captain. He didn't color outside the lines. My slapdash approach to life was a rebellion and then a door to freedom for him, especially in the bedroom.

"Do you want to lick this off?" I had giggled, gesturing to the melting bit of ice cream that had fallen into my cleavage. He'd been staring at it with laser intensity. Little did I know the monster I was about to unleash with that question. That one act—messy, uninhibited and full of laughter—invited him through a door he never wanted to close again. Or so I'd thought until recently.

The sex had been incredible. Justin hadn't been my first, but he'd been the one who listened to me and made an effort to figure out what would drive me crazy. He was the one who'd discovered what would send me over the edge into the kind of orgasm that makes you feel like the world is telescoping in on you. He had a wicked grin and the kind of charisma that somehow talked me into sex in a bathroom at his little sister's bat mitzvah. On vacation in Chicago, I found myself making out with a statuesque brunette. His sexual adventurousness found a matching spirit in my own.

When we'd moved to New York after graduation, he'd

worked crazy hours. When he arrived home, no matter how late, he never failed to pull me to him under the covers. He'd wake me with his mouth, with his fingers, with his cock.

Marriage didn't change a thing for us.

"A sex club. Want to go? We can just watch," he'd murmured as he nuzzled my neck. "Fifteen minutes. If you're not comfortable, we leave. It's our vacation; let's do something crazy."

I'd clutched his hand as we'd entered the building. Justin encouraged me to direct our exploration. Hearing moans of pleasure curved my lips. Compliments directed at my cleavage and my legs assuaged my nerves.

Justin began to give me gentle kisses. Watching a lusty blonde with three men made me wet. Soon we were making out against a wall, Justin's hand darting into my panties to tease my clit.

"I want to do something," he'd said as I widened my stance to give him more access to my pussy.

"What?" I'd asked distractedly, willing to try almost anything if he'd just keep doing that.

"Let me spank you."

My eyes, which had been shut to better focus on the stirring orgasm, flew open. "Why?"

His hand moved from my clit to squeeze my ass. "There's plenty of people here who'd love to spank that ass of yours, but only I can. Let me show off that you're mine. Make them jealous."

"Jealous?" I liked the way the word tasted in my mouth.

"Jealous."

I nodded my consent. Justin led me to the red plush couch and sat down in the middle. He patted the seat next to him. I knelt next to him, allowing him to lower me over his lap. One of his hands braced my body, keeping me balanced. The other slid up and down my legs before lifting my skirt to my waist and exposing my green lacy panties.

I braced, waiting for the strike, but was surprised instead when his fingers slid beneath the lace, dipped into my wet pussy and then danced over my clit. Relaxing into the strokes of his fingers, I let Justin toy with me. I had completely forgotten the public aspect until I heard a strange voice ask if Justin would lower my panties to let him see my cunt. I felt the cool air of the room caress my skin as Justin complied.

"Beautiful girl you have there," the voice said. "Can I?"

"Sorry, she's mine," said Justin just as I'd tensed with worry.

His words relaxed me. Justin wouldn't let anything or anyone hurt me.

Justin's thumb teased my clit. "Do you like knowing you made a stranger hard at the sight of you?"

My body answered his question as I became even wetter. He chuckled, and his hand withdrew. I was wondering what he was going to do next when his palm landed with a sharp smack on my ass.

"Naughty girl, aren't you?" I knew he was checking to see if I wanted to continue.

"Yes," I'd whispered.

"Louder." His voice grew sharper as his hand came down again.

"Yes, I'm your naughty girl. I like it," I'd moaned when a staccato rain of slaps landed.

I was rewarded with long teasing strokes on my clit and a finger plunging into my cunt.

Alternating waves of pain and pleasure: my ass began to burn with the same hot fire that my clit was chasing. *Slap!* "Are you a slut?" *Slap! Slap! Slap!*

"YES!" The reward for the right answer on my clit. My clit would then light on fire with need as my ass cooled, only to be denied just before orgasm.

"Please, Justin..." I begged, my eyes wet with desire and pain.

"What?"

"Let me fuck you," I whimpered.

His hands moved and I was free. Shakily, I stood and reached for the bowl of condoms sitting on a table nearby. A strange hand dipped in and passed me one. I thanked him absently as, transfixed, I watched Justin open his jeans and free his cock.

I straddled and sheathed him, not caring if the entire population of California was watching. Hungrily, I began to ride him, kissing the lips that had been denied me during the spanking. Orgasm flooded me, hitting with the force of a category-five hurricane, sending my hips into a spastic frenzy of motion. Justin groaned as he came moments later.

We were both a bit disoriented as a small spattering of applause signaled that our viewing public knew we were done.

"Thank you," he'd murmured as he'd kissed and praised me in the hotel room that night.

In never forcing and never demanding that I try anything, Justin made it safe to try everything.

Things had changed, though. Maybe it was the move to Asia three years ago. Maybe it was having Liz, and then Adam eleven months later, almost to the day. Apparently breastfeeding wasn't the effective birth control my midwife had billed it to be. Isolation from our friends and family, ten thousand miles and twelve time zones away, hadn't helped. Maybe Singapore, with its rigid social customs and conservatism, was exactly the wrong place to bring Justin; he'd seemed to slip back into that quiet and socially correct armor he'd discarded back in college.

These days, when Justin walked through the door, there were no enthusiastic kisses or gropes. He'd play with our kids as I tried to give an abbreviated recap of the day and reheated his dinner. We'd put the little ones to bed and then he'd want to zone out in front of the TV with me. On weekends, he'd either "pop into work for a few hours" (translation: the whole day) or we'd take the kids out.

In bed, after he thought I'd fallen asleep, I could feel the mattress vibrate as he jerked off to porn on his iPhone. When we did have sex, it was the kind of paint-by-numbers progress of kiss, breast/pussy/cock play, penetration and done rut that I had always sworn we would *never* let ourselves fall into.

Now in the mall, I was a woman on a mission. I started on the top floor and systematically began to shop. Not spending like a woman out for revenge on the husband I felt isolated from (the woman in the mirror would've, and had, gone on that shopping spree at Toys R Us), but instead buying pretty clothes. I studiously ignored shorts and tank tops. I pretended flip-flops didn't exist.

Several thousand dollars and far too many bags to take on a subway car later, I stood in the taxi queue, waiting my turn. Other women had more impressive shopping bags—from Prada, Burberry, Louis Vuitton—but I had more of them, which made me feel triumphant.

Once home, I made my selections from the purchases and packed a suitcase. I kissed my napping toddlers and thanked my helper profusely for her willingness to keep an eye on them overnight.

"To the Conrad Hotel by Suntec City, please?" I asked, as I settled myself in the backseat of the cab.

The room I checked into was a step up from the kind of room we'd always stayed in during college. The kind of room we'd pictured when talking about how one day we'd "really make it and can blow money on nice rooms and sexy trips." The kind of room in which we'd planned to stay in and fuck all day. Sadly, it had been years since we'd stayed in and fucked anywhere, much less a hotel.

I wanted to call Justin.

No. First things first. I put my phone down.

I spent two hours waxing, tweezing, washing and brushing myself into a close approximation of a human female. My new panties and dress reminded me of a femininity I'd forgotten.

I sat down next to a window in a cushioned chair and watched the sun set at seven, contemplating my choices. Divorce. Crappy sex. Great father, but barely noticed me. When had we last laughed together? He'd never cheat on me. Round and round the thoughts went.

At eight, I made the call. Shocked that I wanted him to meet me in a hotel room, Justin left work without protesting and without requesting another hour or three "just to finish this one thing."

When I heard the knock on the door, I still wasn't sure what I wanted to ask for.

"Cara, I don't understand..." he began before he stopped and stared.

He took two steps forward. His hand traced the neckline of the sundress. "What's this? I've never seen this before..."

I stepped back, and the hunger I'd seen building in his eyes fell away as they became dull and distant again. "Justin, we need to talk."

His suit instantly became protective armor. His jaw tightened, but his face relaxed into a neutral expression. If anything, his tie looked tighter. I could have been talking to our accountant. But we'd been together far too long for me to think that what I was seeing was reality. He was anything but detached behind the mask.

I shared my frustration, my isolation and my anger. I got an eyebrow raise in response. When I pointed out how long it had been since he'd given me an orgasm, I thought I saw a small flinch.

"I need more," I blurted out.

"Are you leaving me?" he asked, his voice carefully distant.

"That depends on you."

A short nod, indicating I should continue.

"I used to feel lust when I saw you. I'd look at your hands and fantasize about them sliding under my skirt at that movie we saw on our third date. I'd see your dimples and remember all the stuff you talked me into...remember Cabo? Now it's like you're a stranger. But I'm a stranger, too. I didn't recognize myself in a mirror today. We're two strangers."

I desperately needed him to understand what I wanted.

As I'd talked, Super Corporate Guy had fallen away. Justin had leaned against the wall, hands in his pockets, lips quirking in small smiles at the memories. "Strangers?" He rolled the word around in his mouth, testing its flavor.

"Strangers."

"If you were my wife, I'd tell you that I'd work harder on us. That I love you. But you're a stranger." As he circled me, inhaling my perfume, his voice got deeper.

"That's right. I'm a stranger. And you're here for one reason."

"You're the kind of woman who'd bring a stranger to a hotel room for that?" he asked, his hand sliding over my breast, pinching my nipple for emphasis.

That touch sent a long-missing ripple through my body. I hesitated, hoping he'd remember what I love. The pinch grew harder until I gasped, then changed to a rhythmic back and forth against the erect nub hungry for that exact touch. My eyes closed with pleasure. He leaned forward and began to nibble on my neck, his finger still at work on my breast, his other hand sliding down to cup my ass.

"Yes..." I hissed with pleasure.

Suddenly he was kissing me, and he wasn't a stranger anymore. He was the man I'd loved for more than ten years, and he was playing stranger in the hotel room with me. We were playing. We were connecting. And that sexual heat, which had been banked for who knew how long, came roaring back to life.

I wrapped my hand in his tie, creating a leash, and pulled him to his knees.

"I'm also the kind of woman who wants an orgasm—now." I growled the last word.

He lowered my panties. Justin nudged my legs apart, as I pulled him close. His fingers parted my lips, and his tongue teased my slit, coming close to, but not touching, my clit. I wrapped the tie around my hand again, pulling him tighter and closer. He chuckled, which teased my aching clit even more. Finally he gave it a gentle caress that caused my knees to buckle.

Justin caught me and lowered me to the floor. Pushing the skirt of the sundress to my waist, he returned to my pussy. Teasing, tormenting kisses pushed me to the edge. I could feel the world shrinking to just my cunt and his tongue. I pleaded for release, trying to pull his head closer, to keep him on task, to finish the job.

"You're being naughty," he said. He sat up, and I watched as his hand went to his tie. He slowly and deliberately untied it. "If you can't let me take care of you like a good little slut, I'm going to have to restrain you."

I shivered with delight. "Do what you think you have to."

The dimple I hadn't seen in months appeared as he gave me a smile I'd last seen when we conceived Adam. His hands closed over my wrists, and the soft silk whispered promises as he tied a knot Houdini would've been hard-pressed to escape from. I felt my hands rise over my head with another whisper of silk as I strained to see him tying the other end to the leg of the desk.

He returned his attention to my wet pussy. Lying between my thighs, he took a moment to look at me.

"It's been so long since you let me," he began, almost wistfully, slipping out of character.

"I've never let you do this," I reminded him even as I wondered at his word choice. When was the last time he'd been interested? That he'd asked to go down on me? That he hadn't bothered asking for permission and just woke me up with it?

He nodded and smiled. "Right. But you're going to let me tonight, aren't you?"

"It seems I lack the choice," I teased back, indicating my bonds.

The fabric of the skirt flowed upward and I lay open before him. His tongue began the same pattern of teasing and momentary reward that had buckled my legs when standing. My hips began to undulate. My pelvis moved with his lips and tongue in a dance so well-remembered that even as the steps changed, the partnership was seamless and beautiful.

I closed my eyes and let the pleasure wash through me, building from small lapping waves to roaring tsunamis, threatening to break down any and every barrier I'd erected or let become erected. When I came, the game was over, because it was Justin's name that burst forth.

He gave me a few moments to lie there, senseless, feeling aftershocks ripple through my body. I didn't need to open my eyes to know he was smiling.

"This is new?" he asked, running his fingers contemplatively over the buttons that flowed from neckline to hem of the halter-top sundress.

"Yes," I breathed, barely able to open my eyes.

"I hope you didn't pay much for it," he said. As he did so, he gathered a handful of fabric in each hand and tried to rip it. When the fabric didn't give, he tried again.

"What's this made of? Titanium?" he asked, exasperated.

The failure, rather than darkening the moment, inspired gales of laughter. Laughter had always been one of the ways we connected. More layers of distance peeled away. I began to see not just my lover but my best friend reappearing before my eyes.

"Defeated by a dress," he said finally, still gasping with laughter. He lowered himself to lie next to me.

His hand caressed the length of my still-bound arms. He didn't offer to untie me and I didn't ask him to.

"You might try unbuttoning it," I suggested saucily.

"Indeed," he murmured, clever fingers already at work. "And what have we here? No bra? How scandalous." The last was said with a teasing grin...that had always been his mother's word of choice to describe my braless state.

"You know, you could actually be doing something productive with that smart mouth of yours."

"Like apologizing?" His hand slipped in and fondled my breast, playing his thumb over my nipples. He remembered how sensitive they were postorgasm.

"I have a feeling that might be a mutual activity. I haven't really been there for you all that much lately, either."

He kissed me gently at first, his lips barely brushing mine. Changing the angle, he deepened the kiss, tongue flicking out to caress my lips, persuading them to give him entry. His hand caressed my cheek and slid into my hair as he kissed me with every ounce of passion I'd thought he'd lost for me. I returned it with the same urgency and ardent desire.

"There you are," I whispered.

"Here I am," he agreed. "I love you, Cara."

"I love you, too, Justin," I said. "Make love with me."

He smiled and whispered in my ear, "I hope you brought a condom. I love those two, but I'm not up for number three. Since I apparently have super sperm or you have slutty eggs, I'm scared of going commando."

"Look in the drawer."

The extra-large box made him laugh again. "I hope you weren't planning to use all of these tonight. You'd wring me dry, woman."

"They're a promise." I met his eyes.

"To..."

"To make an effort not to lose this again," I responded.

"I like that promise," he replied, returning to the floor with the box nearby. "Now prepare to be ravished," he said in a fake pirate accent.

He began by nuzzling my neck as his hands made short work of the last few buttons on my dress. He took his time, exploring every inch of skin, making me sigh and moan. My frustration mounted. With the exception of his tie, he was still fully dressed.

The starched cotton of his shirt was at odds with the softness of his hands. He used the contrast to his advantage, intent on the task at hand. I could feel his cock straining toward freedom but could do nothing besides beg for him to do me, and arch my hips. I was told that I'd done without pleasure for too long and he'd do me only after I'd come several more times.

His fingers slipped between my thighs, dipping into my hot core, testing and teasing until he found my G-spot. Massaging it, he reminded me of sexy times from our past. "Do you remember when we played miniature golf for your panties? The hand job you gave me as you were driving that rented sports car down Highway 1? The Petite Theatre in Paris? The time you flashed the window girl in Amsterdam?"

The waves of sexy memories danced in time with his fingers. The familiar pressure built again. When it broke, I heard an audible crash and saw I'd moved the heavy wood desk just enough for the phone to have fallen off.

I couldn't help it. The laughter bubbled up in me, and when our eyes met, I couldn't keep it stifled any longer. He buried his face in my shoulder and laughed with me. We each would calm down a little, but the second our eyes met, we'd start laughing again.

Shaking his head, Justin got up to hang up the receiver and place the phone back on the desk. It rang. He frowned and picked it up.

"Hello? No, everything's fine." The wicked smile returned. "Just making love to my gorgeous wife. Good night."

If it hadn't already felt like I was floating a few inches above my body, I would have sworn I'd just had an out-of-body experience. My proper workaholic husband had just bragged to a stranger that he was doing me?

"You've been just as lost as I've been," I said, the light dawning.

He untied my hands and picked me up to move me gently to the bed.

"Yes. I saw how hard it was with the baby. Then just as stuff looked like it was settling down with Liz, you got pregnant again. I figured the best thing I could do was be a good dad and help out. Not be another strain on you. I know you don't get enough sleep. I figured sex was the last thing you'd want to use energy on, all things considered. It's not like there's a shortage of work for me to do. It was easier to focus on work," he said.

"I thought you just didn't want me anymore because I looked like a mess and..." My voice trailed off.

"Baby, there isn't a day when I don't want you. I think you should eat something—you're too skinny," and here he nipped my hip bone. "These are sharp, but I want you as much as I ever have—more."

"I want you, too," I said, slowly unbuttoning his shirt, kissing each inch of skin as it became exposed.

"Cara," he whispered, and then moaned, "Cara," as my tongue flicked across a dark nipple.

I opened the buttons at his wrists and pushed the shirt from his shoulders. Encouraging him to lie down, I straddled his hips, feeling his cock hard beneath his dress slacks. I played with his chest hair, stroking it, tugging it, kissing down the love trail it made from his chest to his waistband. I licked his earlobes, his neck, and his nipples.

I took one of his hands and, meeting his eyes, began to suck his middle finger, taking its full length into my mouth. Beneath me, his cock jumped in echoing need. I rolled my hips to tease him as I sucked the finger.

"Cara," he moaned, dragging out the second syllable like a prayer.

I moved to kneel beside him and unbuckled his belt. His hands fisted in the duvet as I took my time with the waistband and inched down his zipper. His cock strained to break free of his boxers. He arched his hips.

I smiled as I stroked him through his boxers.

"Cara, I'm not Superman," he moaned.

As I slid down his pants and boxers, his cock sprung free to demand its fair share of attention. Taking his cock in hand, I bent to lick the head, swirling my tongue around it. Justin swore with pleasure as he fought the urge to come. I fondled his balls as I licked my way down and then back up his shaft. A finger slipped back to tease and press on his taint, as I took the head of his cock and then the shaft into my mouth. I could feel my pussy throbbing in need, demanding the same thing Justin was.

An expert multitasker, I opened the box of condoms and extracted one. I replaced my mouth with the condom before straddling Justin. Our eyes locked as I lowered myself onto him. I felt my body happily accept his cock, and my eyes closed with pleasure.

I let instinct and need take over, rocking my hips slowly and then more urgently. I positioned my body to best stimulate my G-spot, knowing Justin would only let himself come once I had. As if it had only been moments instead of months, my body knew exactly the right rhythm, the right pace to let the orgasm build and then flood my body. Moments after I began to moan his name, I heard Justin gasp mine as he came.

I let my body still, and we were motionless for a few moments, letting pleasant aftershocks dash through our bodies. Then I gingerly lifted myself off him, careful to keep the condom in place. He was equally cautious in removing it, both of us treating the sperm like potentially dangerous prisoners.

Lying in the king-size bed, we talked and laughed long into the night. In the morning, Justin called in sick, and we spent the morning in bed renewing our commitment to each other. When it was time to check out, we headed home to our children, eager to find the balance between his work, our own interests, our love, our lust and our family...with maybe a sandwich or two for me in there somewhere.

THE NETHERLANDS

Justine Elyot

These were the things I thought of when Matthew told me he was taking me to Amsterdam: tulips, windmills, canals, Van Gogh, dope, sex trafficking.

If you work for the Dutch Tourist Board, please forgive me. I know the list is hackneyed now, but I didn't then. Oh, how experience has skewed my view now. Tulips are off the list; windmills have sailed right out of the running. The sex remains, but without the trafficking. Where is it on my list now? Much higher up. I'll explain.

Our relationship was a year old when the choir took its biennial exchange visit to Amsterdam. Matthew was the chorus master. I was in the chorus. I suppose that made him my master from the moment I passed the audition, though he only became so in the more intimate sense some months later.

I was a D/s neophyte at the time, knowing what I knew only from *The Story of O* and some Depeche Mode lyrics, so Matthew taught me a great deal in a short space of time. He was never less than careful of my feelings and considerate of my boundaries; had I known that a man who loved so dearly to wield a whip could be so *gentle*, perhaps I would have plunged into this kind of relationship before. But, echoing my Amsterdam checklist, my concept of a dominant man had been a jumble of rather frightening and ridiculous stereotypes, so I had written it off as masturbation fantasy.

More fool me? Perhaps. But on the other hand, I could not regret waiting for the right man. And Matthew was certainly the right man for me.

The morning after our performance of Bach's *St. John Passion* in the St. Nicolaaskerk, Matthew and I visited the Rijksmuseum.

We were queuing in the ticket hall when Matthew's phone bleeped and he read the message. He bit his lip and glanced sideways at me.

"Who is it?" I asked.

"Do you remember me telling you about my friends Jan and Karin?"

"Oh! *Those* friends."

"Yes. *Those* friends. They've invited us for lunch." He put his phone in his pocket and wrapped a hand around my elbow, leaning down to murmur in my ear. "They'd very much like to meet you."

My scalp prickled and the room swam before my eyes. Had that time come? Was I ready? How do you know when you're ready?

Harvesting all the breath I could from my tightened chest, I essayed a tone that was several shades lighter than I felt.

"Is this the kind of meeting that involves nudity?"

He patted my bottom discreetly and said, "Only if you want it to be, Loveday. You know that."

"Right."

We were at the desk. We bought our tickets and wandered up the stairs to the first-floor galleries, though I had no clue where we were going, and if Matthew hadn't been leading the way, I could just as easily have walked through an open window. Dutch Renaissance art was approximately the last thing on my mind.

We had discussed this. When I felt safe, when the time was right, when the trust was there, perhaps we could dip our toes into the "scene"—although, in reality, it would only be me doing the toe-dipping. Before we met, Matthew had been an accomplished scene player, in great demand wherever his international conducting career took him. He had belonged to an exclusive members' club, discretion assured, global contacts and all that. In my mind, it was all terribly glamorous, but also extremely intimidating. The women were sophisticated beauties. The men were power brokers and business magnates. Everything took place in gigantic drawing rooms full of dark wood and oxblood leather. And they all sipped brandy all the time.

I thought back to what Matthew had told me about Jan and Karin, but I couldn't remember much. Karin liked to switch... was that her? Or was that the one in Hamburg? I often asked him about his adventures in BDSM, usually while we were in the bath and, while he never avoided the issue, he always did his best to ensure that I wasn't left feeling inadequate or second best. *"You have to remember, Loveday, that none of those women were really 'mine' in the way that you are. Having you, the way I do, is what I have always wanted. I wouldn't swap it for all the scenes in the world."*

I glowed at the memory, smiling as Matthew nudged me down on to a bench.

"So what do you think?" he said.

"Of?"

"*The Night Watch.*"

I realized for the first time that we were seated directly in front of Rembrandt's huge masterpiece.

"Oh! Yes, it's...big, isn't it?"

He snorted, then took my hand and placed it in his lap, stroking it.

"We don't have to go. You don't have to do anything. I'll fob them off and take you on a canal boat instead..."

"No, I..." I looked away from the ruffed and feather-hatted Dutchmen and up to my suited and booted choirmaster. "I think I want to meet them. I think I could give it a go."

He looked at me for a long time. I think the other people in the gallery must have wondered why we'd bothered to pay the entrance fee.

"If you're sure," he said at last. "And *only* if you're sure. The minute you aren't happy, we can leave."

I nodded. "I know. I trust you, see."

He kissed the top of my head. "I'll try to be worthy of it. Shall we come back here tomorrow? I want to take you back to the hotel and dress you for the occasion."

The look on his face was worth the trepidation. I had handed him a key and now he was ready to dive into the treasure box. It would be all right. If I was with him, it would be all right.

Jan and Karin lived in one of the tall, narrow old merchants' houses facing onto the Prinsengracht canal.

"They can't be short of a bob or two," I shivered to Matthew, looking up at the huge windows, like mournful cartoon eyes with flower tubs rimming the lower lids. "Dressing me for the occasion" had not been synonymous with "dressing me for the weather." Beneath my long wool coat, I wore my evening concert dress—a long silk sheath with crystal beading—and beneath that only stockings and suspenders. My high heels were not suitable for either the early hour or the cobbled towpath, so I drew plenty of attention on our short journey, mostly of the nudge-wink-whisper variety. Matthew seemed splendidly happy with this, so I worked it, tottering proudly in my stilettos, hand in hand with my adored master. I imagined myself being brought as a gift, which I was, in a way. I was wrapped up and ribbon-tied in my submission before we even arrived.

"They're well off," Matthew confirmed, ringing the doorbell. "I told you Karin was a film producer, didn't I?"

"No!"

"Oh, sorry, thought I did."

"Maybe you did." I wrung my hands, nervous enough to vomit on the doormat. "It's all a blur. All these people. All these stories."

He put a reassuring hand on the small of my back.

"You're shaking. You don't have to worry. Just follow my lead. You can say no at any time. There won't be any judgment or any more said about it."

The door was opened by a woman. I registered a bright white smile and even brighter red hair, and that was all I could hang my focus on as she chatted to Matthew, leading us along a dark wood corridor and up some stairs.

I concentrated on the warmth and familiarity of his hand on mine, leading me upward, as Karin told us how much she and Jan were looking forward to this and how happy they were for Matthew that he had found what she called a "soul mate." My nerves dissolved a little at that. It was a sweet thing to say.

The upstairs room in which we were to take our lunch was...normal. I flicked my eyes to its four corners while Jan and Matthew clapped backs and hailed each other in a hearty, mannish way, but there was no sign of a whip or a chain. Not even a bottle of brandy.

"And you must be Loveday?" Jan had one of those booming, jovial voices, accent thicker than lard. I could not imagine it giving the sex orders in Matthew's precise and unequivocal fashion. He had kind blue eyes that crinkled at the corners, thinning blond hair and that hulking all-shoulders build. In his leather waistcoat and thong necklaces, he looked like an aging hippie, more at home smoking a joint in one of the red-light district cafés than orchestrating and fine-tuning a submissive's exquisite humiliation. Still, if Matthew rated him...

He almost shook my hand off. I could only smile and nod.

He knows what I am. They both know. Everyone knows here. Everyone knows what I like to have done to me.

The thought was a rush, an unexpected wave of lust knocking me off my skyscraper heels. Even if none of them touched me today, the fact that they knew how I liked to be touched in advance was a concept more erotically potent than anything I had faced before.

"Matthew says you sing like an angel." Karin smiled. She had a warm smile that shone right through my unease and melted it.

"Oh, y'know..." I did the usual modest shruggy thing.

"I would love to hear you sing," said Jan.

"Oh, I don't know..."

"Yes," said Matthew, incisive, cutting through my fluster. "Sing for us."

There was my answer. Matthew said sing. I would sing.

"What shall I do?" I asked him, following him to an upright piano tucked into an alcove.

"Something you feel," he said.

I sang Gounod's "Serenade." At first there was a perceptual dissonance in singing this beautiful, sensual song in this high-windowed Dutch apartment for an audience of kinksters, but Matthew's rippling piano accompaniment and the loving words pulled me into the music's magic and I began to revel in that symbiotic relationship of singer and accompanist, picking up and playing off each other's energies, just as we did outside our musical lives.

Jan and Karin applauded and showered me with embarrassingly fulsome praise while Matthew stood behind me, his hands on my shoulders, as if afraid I might fly up to the ceiling like a helium balloon. I'll admit, I might well have done. Singing always has that effect on me.

"She is amazing, Matthew," said Jan, and suddenly I was aware of the switch. They were not going to talk to me anymore. From now on, I was to be talked about.

"What a wonderful choice you have made. But the lunch is almost ready and I am wondering whether she will eat with us, or would she prefer to serve?"

Matthew's fingers tightened on my shoulders. The word "serve" had precipitated a stomach flutter and I wanted to press my thighs together, to catch the melting dew settling upon them.

"Well?" Matthew bent to whisper the word in my ear. I knew what he wanted. And I wanted it, too. Jan and Karin looked so touchingly excited. Matthew would be so proud of me. And I would enjoy it! The decision went from complex to elegantly simple in one moment.

"I would like to serve," I said softly.

Karin beamed from ear to ear, extended her hand and led me away into the kitchen.

Over my shoulder, I caught sight of Matthew sinking down into a leather armchair opposite Jan. *Time for the brandy to come out*, I thought with a giddy thrill.

"Okay, so, Loveday," said Karin, shutting the kitchen door behind us. "I haven't heard that name before."

"I'm from Cornwall."

"Oh, yes, Lands End, right?"

"Near there."

The counter was loaded with plates of cold meats, cheeses, dark breads and crackers, pickled fish and varied condiments.

"It's a simple lunch, you see," she said. "And your job is simple. You just bring in the food, pour the drinks and do as you're told." She grinned and squeezed my hand. "You like to do as you're told, right?"

"Some of the time," I said nervously. It was odd to be standing in a kitchen chatting about submission with a total stranger. My skin prickled.

"Well, I know Matthew likes to give orders *all* of the time, so if you're with him..." She winked and that toothpaste-bright smile flashed again.

"How well do you know him? Have you...?"

"We've played together a couple times." She sounded offhand about it all. "He is one of my favorite doms to play with, actually. He's taught Jan a few things."

"That's one thing he's good at," I said with feeling. "Teaching."

"Just one?"

"Well, he's good at lots of things, of course. But that one in particular."

"Listen, before I go back out there, I need to know you are comfortable with this. Are you?"

"Aren't you serving, too?"

"No, I'm a switch. Today I want to enjoy my lunch and have some fun with you. Is that okay?"

I drew a few breaths. Was it okay for this vibrant, confident woman to have fun with me? Yes. Yes, it was.

"So...I just take out the plates and, like, obey orders?"

"That's about it. Oh, and one more thing. You should take off your dress."

My dropped jaw was wasted on her. She had breezed out of the kitchen, leaving me to slip out of the concert gown and stand, nipples to attention, in the middle of the tiled floor. There was no mirror in there, so I leant over and checked myself in the few chrome fittings I could find. I looked flushed and scared. My fingers twisted the silver knot at the center of my choker—more elegant than a collar, but no different in its significance. Engraved on the inside were the words PROPERTY OF M J HARDY.

The food stood silently, forcing its presence on me, reminding me what I was to do. I held myself straight and picked up two platters, balancing them on my palms the way I learned to that summer I waitressed at the bay.

I opened the kitchen door with my bare bottom and spun around to face the audience, who were seated at a long table at the back of the room, blessedly far away from the floor-to-ceiling windows, chatting. They didn't stop when I entered the room. They didn't even look at me until I placed the food down in front of them, and then it was only to cast their eyes up and down me and watch casually while I returned for the remainder of the repast.

I had to pass the platters around while they took what they wanted, still ignoring me, and refill their glasses. I was so intent on doing a good job that I forgot I was naked, until they had all been served and I was instructed by Karin to stand at the end of the table with my hands by my sides and wait until I was needed.

Waiting isn't easy for me. I want to know what is coming,

whether it's a whipping or an orgasm. Anticipation treads a fine line between pleasure and torment. I kept trying to catch Matthew's eye, and I managed it a couple of times, but he looked away immediately and talked more about people they knew, places they'd been, things they'd bought.

I stood there for ten minutes, chest out, thighs clamped together, before Karin took pity on me.

"Come over here," she ordered. "Kneel."

I fell to my knees beside her chair.

"You like cheese? Eat."

She hand-fed me scraps from her plate, pushing her fingers inside my mouth with each morsel, then she made me lick the salty juices from them.

"She's hungry. Greedy girl," she mocked. "Is she a greedy girl, Matthew?"

"Not just for food," he said.

I bowed my head, not wanting Karin to see the rush of red to my cheeks, but she took my chin and forced it up, smiling down delightedly.

"That's great," she said. "She needs a lot of attention. Well, we can give that, can't we?"

"Indeed." I could see Matthew from the corner of my eye, and he was smiling. Beaming, in fact.

Jan wiped his mouth and fingers with a paper napkin, then beckoned me.

"Send her over, Karin," he said. "I want to have a good look at her."

He looked briefly over at Matthew, as if seeking permission, but Matthew didn't flinch. Permission was implicit. They could all do what they wanted with me.

I trotted over to Jan's side; he reached up and tweaked the knot of my choker.

"Is she collared?" he asked Matthew.

"Six months ago."

"Lovely tits. I don't like this silicone thing, do you? I prefer them natural. I always think those silicone tits would be no fun to slap."

Jan demonstrated with a breathtakingly quick sideways swipe, causing my left breast to swing.

"These, on the other hand..." he said, and chuckled. He pinched my nipples, just because it seemed the thing to do, then moved his palm down to cover my shaved mons. "Do you shave her, Matthew? Or does she do it?"

"She usually goes and gets it done professionally. I did it the first time, though."

"It's nice. Turn around."

It took me a second or two to realize I was being directly addressed. A slap to my bare thigh woke me up, and I turned my back to him.

I felt rough hands cup my buttocks, squeezing into them with the thumbs. I sucked in my breath a little; I had leftover bruises from a paddling a couple of days back.

"You had to punish her, Matthew?"

"I'm afraid so. She isn't always this docile, you know."

"Tut tut. What did you use?"

"Wooden hairbrush."

"Hers?"

"Yes."

"Ah, I always think that's a nice touch. She'll think of it every time she brushes her hair."

"That's the reasoning behind it, certainly."

Matthew's voice was very low, lower than usual, and slightly hoarse. I smiled to myself, knowing that this was driving him wild.

"And between those legs..." pondered Jan. "Do you mind?"

"Be my guest." Matthew could barely form words.

Jan's hand parted my thighs.

"Bend over," he ordered roughly, then he pressed hard fingers between my lower lips, swishing them around in my incriminating wetness.

"God, she is very wet," he informed the room.

"Can I see?" Karin rose from her chair and crouched behind me. I felt her warm breath travel over my clit. Jan's fingers prodded and pressed and I bore down on them, looking for the firmest of touches. He took the fingers away and smacked my bum instead.

"Dirty girl," laughed Karin. "You are right, Matthew, she has a greedy pussy."

"Okay." Jan pulled me upright by an elbow. "We have had lunch. Now, dessert. Clear the table, then come back and lie down on it."

My walk back to the kitchen with the empty plates was a tottery one. My thighs were steaming wet and I tingled from head to toe. It was like standing at the top of a very tall slide, wondering if you dare let go and take that ride. I'd let go, I was on the ride and now I couldn't stop until I hit the bottom.

When I came back, I wanted Matthew to help me onto the table, and that familiar contact, his hand on my arm, strengthened me. He felt so sure, so free of doubt. The confidence was infectious, and when I lay flat, legs parted, arms over my head, and looked up at him, I couldn't help but smile into his intense gaze.

He stroked my hair then stood back, waiting for Jan or Karin to dictate the next move.

"I want my dessert," said Karin. "How does she taste?"

"Why don't you sample her?" suggested Matthew. He and

Jan moved to the head of the table and held me down, staring into my eyes while Karin bent over the foot end and slid her face farther and farther toward my widespread cunt.

When her tongue hit my split, I squirmed and sighed, and the men's grip on me tightened accordingly. Karin scooped her tongue around my clit, feathering and dabbing, knowing how to eat me, and Jan was inspired to take advantage of his positioning to give my left breast some of the same treatment. Matthew followed his lead and did the same to my right, still pinning me down at the wrist.

The sensations were exquisite; I felt like I was being devoured from the outside in, and I bucked hard, or as hard as I could while restrained by four strong hands.

The tip of Karin's tongue poked itself inside my cunt while her busy fingers strummed on my clit; the men nipped and chewed at my nipples.

"Oh, please, may I come?" I wailed, remembering just in time the necessity for permission.

There was no answer. It seemed Jan and Karin were waiting for Matthew.

I tried to convey the urgency of my request by pushing my nipple farther into his mouth. He released it and said, "No," quite distinctly, before taking my mouth in a ravenous kiss, drowning out my moan of despair.

"I don't think she's happy with that." Karin was laughing, moving around the table, waiting for Matthew to free my lips so she could replace his with hers.

She plunged her tongue deep inside me, giving me that taste of myself.

"Poor thing," she crooned, stroking my breasts. "She needs it."

"Let's flog her," said Jan hopefully, looking at Matthew, who nodded.

While Karin went off to fetch the instruments of my discipline, Matthew climbed onto the table and positioned himself so that he knelt behind my head, his knees touching my ears. As Karin returned, he leant forward over my body and grabbed my calves, lifting them, pulling them back until he held me by the ankles, keeping me spread open, my bottom cheeks raised off the table so that my coccyx remained in contact with the wood.

Karin and Jan made a big show of deciding which implements to use while Matthew looked down at me from above.

"Be brave," he whispered. "I'm so proud of you."

"I love you," I mouthed back.

He winked then looked up at the others, who were signaling their readiness to begin. They both wielded suede-tailed floggers, favorites for a lengthy erotic spanking, and I relaxed my body, preparing myself for the first stingy swish.

Jan and Karin alternated strokes, laying them hard and fast so that my bottom heated up rapidly. I panted and puffed into Matthew's face, my legs struggling but held firm in his grasp, my hands tempted to stray down and shield my bottom as the burn grew.

Matthew sensed this, I think, and ordered, "Touch yourself."

"Touch...ooooh...myself?"

"Yes. Make yourself come. And don't shut your eyes. I want you to look at me."

"Oh, nice touch," said Jan admiringly, flicking the fiery suede tails back and forth across my bottom.

I reached down and thrummed my clit, keeping my eyes fixed on Matthew, who had put on his particularly stern face, because he knew how that always spurred me on.

Jan and Karin, at the whipping end, chatted to each other,

complimenting themselves on their technique, discussing the particular colors of my flogged bottom and the way I was dripping onto their table.

"You'll lick it off afterward," Karin warned me and I groaned, working my fingers faster, watching the corners of Matthew's lips curl slowly upward.

I'd been ordered to make myself come, but it is always hard to concentrate when I'm taking a whipping; the pain and pleasure bounce around in my brain, crossing each other, colliding, becoming one, then dividing again.

"Harder," hissed Matthew, his eyes narrow, his lips stretched over his teeth. "Whip her harder."

My ass was throbbing now and my clit was fat, round and red, like the Edam cheese I'd sliced earlier. Jan and Karin flicked the floggers in between my bumcheeks, finding the most sensitive spots, ensuring that I would not be able to escape the feeling of soreness for a day or two. The pain became pleasure, every part of me captured and used and taken, and I flooded with orgasm, my eyes trapped open under Matthew's, forced to have every second of my shameful rapture watched and assessed.

He leant down and kissed me again, a kiss of triumph and love and pride, before releasing my ankles and climbing off the table. The three of them lolled in their chairs, drinking coffee, while I serviced each one orally, starting with Karin, finishing with Matthew.

Then, face smeared with juices, mouth tasting of semen, I was sent to the piano to sing again.

Later, standing on a bridge over the canal, Matthew and I stared, hand in hand, down at the water and the pleasure boats that rippled it on their carefree voyages.

"You were brilliant," he said. "Outstanding. What did you think?"

"It was amazing. Really, such an incredible rush. Not sure I could do it all the time though. It's one of those things that's probably best in moderation."

Matthew nodded sagely. "Yes. I think I agree with you. A special treat, for high days and holidays. And choir tours."

"How many of those do we have booked?"

He grinned down at me rakishly.

"How many would you like?"

We've been on a few since then. They are an ornament to our relationship rather than integral to its function—we are, essentially, a duet rather than an ensemble. The desire for ornamentation in life has led to many wonderful things, all the same: *The Night Watch,* choral music, kinky sex.

And I never think of tulips anymore when Amsterdam is mentioned.

PREDATORY
TREE

Craig J. Sorensen

D awn sunlight made cookie-cutter outlines of the arts and
crafts window on the green blazer from Cathie's new job at
Jack Harkin Real Estate.

The alarm was not ringing. Sean tried to calculate why he
was awake.

Brappa!

His head lifted from the satin-wrapped pillow.

Brrrappa! Brrrrrappa bzzzzzz!

He looked back to Cathie for a reaction. Her pale blue eyes
looked through his skull. He waved his hand in front of her
face. Nothing. He remembered the first time she had done this
so many years before. It was the morning of the rose-flooded
cathedral wedding that her father had taken out a second mort-
gage to provide. Sean had been sure something was wrong
and grabbed her shoulder. The memory of her blood-curdling
scream put a chill up his spine even now as the sounds outside
the window consolidated.

Bzzzzz chhhrrrr! KHHHRRRRT!

Blood rushed between Sean's legs. The grinding sound seemed to stroke the core of his spine like a strong hand on a cock. He reached to within a micron of Cathie's warm arm then eased toward her shoulder. They hadn't made love in so long. He needed to feel her.

Woodchip spittle hissed like a fountain amidst the chain-saw's belching motor. Cathie remained still as death except for the almost imperceptible rise and fall of her chest. He finally curled his hand into a ball and retreated.

His cock ached. He leaned close to her ear and whispered. "Close your eyes, Cathie. Please?" She was motionless, staring.

He folded his hard-on into his underwear and got up as the chainsaw's sounds became more insistent. He looked one more time into Cathie's blank, open eyes, then went into the bath-room to get an early start on the workday.

Cathie stood, hips against the counter, with the whisper of a potato peeler tossing brown curls in the stainless sink. "Hi, honey, how was the traffic?"

"Sucked. Getting worse and worse." Sean hung his keys on the peg next to a photograph of Samantha when she was a little girl. It didn't matter how many times he looked at the photo, his heart always raced as if it was just yesterday that he walked into the backyard to see Cathie, her camera pointed toward the tree. Samantha was so high in the huge maple that it made him dizzy. He almost screamed out, but fear that he might startle the girl and send her plummeting silenced him. He squeezed Cathie's shoulder. Samantha's scabbed knees clung to the branch as she grinned upside down. Sean pleaded with Cathie to get her down. "She'll be fine. Like mother, like daughter." Cathie rolled her shoulder from Sean's grip and shot a couple more pictures.

Sean held his breath until Samantha scaled down the tree like a squirrel.

Sean shook off the memory and leaned with his back to the counter. He brushed Cathie's long hair from the side of her face. "You did it again."

"Did what?"

Sean widened his eyes and cocked his head like he was sleeping.

"Stop it, Sean, I don't sleep with my eyes open."

"Yes, you do."

"I don't!"

He wretched out a crackling snore.

"And I don't snore!"

"No, you don't snore," he agreed with a bob of his eyebrows. He turned around and looked into the backyard.

"I had a long day, Sean."

"Mmm?" He squinted. Something was missing. Something big. Huge.

Cathie continued, "I'm not sure about—"

Sean leaned toward the window. "Holy shit!"

"What?" She followed his eyes.

"It's that beautiful old oak in Gary's yard they were cutting down this morning. There isn't a goddamned thing wrong with that tree." Branches and limbs were scattered knee deep across Gary's manicured lawn.

"Maybe he's pruning it."

"You don't cut a tree like that to prune it." Sean felt like a WWII vet looking around the empty ballroom at the sixty-fifth reunion. He rushed out and positioned himself on the fence near where Gary surveyed the carnage. Gary shrugged. "Look, the way it hangs, if lightning were to hit it and it fell over, it might—"

"That tree was older than we are, Gary."

"Yeah, and its time had come."

Sean lurched back on the fence like taking a .44 slug. There were a thousand things he wanted to say. His jaw fell slack. He climbed down from the fence and walked slowly back to the house.

Cathie's ease with herself sometimes made her easy to overlook, like walking through a beautiful garden every morning, or seeing a beautiful tree out the back window every evening. Sean stepped from his morning shower and draped a towel on his hips. She stood casually, her long nude body still a bit damp. She combed her silver-tinted, bright-red hair, then slathered face cream on her fingers. He set to shaving as she rubbed the cream on her freckled cheeks then wiped the remainder over her silky stretch marks, the last bit deposited beneath the border of her vibrant pubic hair, as she had done for years.

She smiled then walked into the bedroom and he heard the closet open. He continued his routine.

Brappa.

Sadness filled Sean.

Brappa, brappa.

Mourning to desperation, he bit his lip so hard it hurt.

Brappa bzzzzzzz!

His towel rose like a drawbridge. He felt that strange, desperate desire again. He tilted his torso and looked into the bedroom. Cathie was an exception to the widely held notion that women take forever to get ready. For once, he was disappointed in this. She was already fully dressed, making final adjustments to the green blazer. She fanned her wet hair out. She looked back at Sean and blew a kiss, then started for the stairs. "Have a nice day, sweetie."

He wanted to yell, *Wait, Cathie!* It came out, "Have a good day."

Her high heels clacked down the oak staircase. His cock throbbed as the chainsaw continued to churn. He stroked his rod a couple of times and thought about bringing himself off, but the clock informed him that he had no time for such luxury. He couldn't afford to be even ten minutes late these days.

Cathie brought a second helping of spaghetti. He never had to ask. She ladled the extra sauce he always wanted over it and pushed the grated parmigiano-reggiano closer to his hand. Sean seasoned then twirled the pasta and scooped extra sauce. "Thanks, Cathie."

She smiled and nodded. Her smile faded slowly as she traced down one lapel of her Jack Harkin blazer. "You'd think selling houses would be easy the way the town is growing and—"

Sean took a bite. His mind drifted. Ivy League tuition for one daughter, the other now ready to marry a man he hated. Skyrocketing real estate taxes, a dot-com bust alumnus boss, nicknamed "the kid," who wore flip-flops and nu metal T-shirts, firmly convinced that youth and unspeakably long hours were the only answer to success. This, combined with the threat of draconian layoffs and not another job in sight. Sean shook his head to clear his thoughts momentarily. "What was that?" He twirled another bite of spaghetti.

"You okay, hon?"

"Oh, yeah, I'm fine."

Cathie stroked the stubble on his cheek. "You sure?"

"Yeah, I'm fine, Cathie. What were you saying?"

She smiled. "Nothing. What's wrong?"

"Today I became absolutely sure 'the kid' has it out for me..."

Cathie leaned forward and rested her chin on her palm. She nodded for him to continue.

Sean and Cathie sat out on the back porch, he in sweats, she still in her outfit from work. He pointed to the heap of rough-cut limbs and trunk pieces in the neighbor's yard. "Cathie, if they keep taking the trees down, this neighborhood will look like one of those popcorn cul-de-sacs out by the freeway. I mean, they've taken out seven trees this year, and every goddamned one that's been cut down was perfectly healthy. Seven fucking trees!" He methodically pointed at the spots where the trees had once been. "You'd think they were all plotting to get us. Fucking predatory trees!"

Cathie laughed and cupped her hand gently in his. She turned her head deliberately at the thickening stripe of bare limbs in the center of the old maple in their own backyard. He followed her eyes. "It's perfectly healthy." He didn't want to go there again.

Cathie tilted her head sympathetically. "Sean, it looks like hell. We can always grow a new tree. Trees are good like that." She laughed, but her voice trailed off when Sean didn't join in. She drew a deep breath. "Really, we could plant a new one," she offered softly.

"Sam loves this tree, Cathie."

"Sam loves to climb. She climbs anything that will stand still for her. And she'll have trees of her own soon enough after she marries...him." Cathie sighed and rolled her eyes. "Anyway, is all this really about trees? I never knew you cared so much about them."

"Oh sure. I mean, I love trees, you know?" Sean's mind again faded into worries. "But speaking of climbing, 'the kid' really pissed me off today. He doesn't know shit about the business. He thinks he's smarter than everyone around him. He proposes ideas that we've tried a dozen ways and proven won't work, and still everyone just licks his fucking boots. 'Great idea, Brad!' Fuck, I just don't know."

Cathie's expression invited him to continue. He opened his mouth. The strange sensation he'd gotten looking in her eyes, wide in sleep that first chainsaw morning, swelled in the back of his mind. Cutting: the sound of cutting, of severance. Loss.

It was rare that Cathie slept with her eyes open. Those times played in his head: That time Sam's fever spiked so high. The day Cathie wrecked her car. The flooded basement and all those precious books her grandmother had left her. When her youngest sister's husband died so suddenly.

"Go on, Sean."

He focused. "So how's *your* new job going?"

Cathie leaned back. "What?"

"How're things at Jack Harkin?" He smoothed the lapel of her blazer.

"Oh, that's fine." She gave a dismissive wave.

"Really?"

"Oh, you bet. I mean, there are always growing pains. You were saying? About 'the kid'?"

"What growing pains?" He patted her thigh.

She tilted her head softly. "Well, I guess it wasn't what I expected, or maybe I didn't know what to expect. I—I really don't know if I'm cut out—" She held up her wrist to her forehead like she was checking for a fever. "Look, I'm fine. It's all good."

"Keep going." He stroked her cheek, then rubbed her lip with his thumb like it was a magic lamp and this was what he needed to do to get the genie out. His eyes drifted to the yard.

"What was that about 'the kid'? His name is Brad? Didn't know—"

He forced his eyes away from the naked middle of the tree back to Cathie. "What about your job?"

Cathie's carefully crafted smile washed out like low tide. "Oh, Sean, I don't think I'm going to be able to cut it. I'm not making sales. I'm so afraid of letting them down, worse still, letting you down. I know you're having troubles at work and...well...anyway..." She left a gap for him to speak. It was a long gap.

To Sean, this silence, where not even a bird song could be heard, spoke volumes. "My work is fine. Keep going."

A tear trickled down each of her cheeks and she dried them up quickly with one thumb. "I'm fine." Her lip quivered. She turned away.

All the years she had been there for him. She never seemed to worry, never seemed troubled, but he wondered how many times he'd really listened. He'd never seen her cry, even when she broke her leg or when they set it. He recalled the mornings along the way, looking into her occasional blank sleeping stares. Through them all, she always listened. Her earnest listening seemed to make life so much easier.

"I'm here for you. We'll work it out." He placed his palm delicately on her forearm.

"Oh shit, Sean." She turned back and grabbed ahold of his neck. She pulled her chair up on two legs as she drew close to him.

"What?"

Tears gushed down her sharp jawbone. Her sobs were loud, like a chainsaw.

"What?"

She held tight to his neck and continued. She cried so hard he knew he'd made a huge mistake. The only thing he could do was hold her tight while she soaked the front of his shirt. She finished and stood up. He stood up with her and she held up her hand. "I need some time alone."

She was already asleep, curled in the fetal position, still in her work clothes right down to green high heels when he found her in the bedroom. He cupped tight to her back and held her. She slept on. She was sleeping so deeply. He lay awake half the night wondering what he had done, hoping that by holding still and cradling her he could make it right.

A strip of pale light brought sparks of color to the bedroom. Sean listened to a breeze that made whispers of the defiant leaves that soldiered on in the old maple in the backyard. He didn't know what awoke him.

No chainsaw.

He turned over toward Cathie. Her body was sprawled atop the covers in the clothes she'd worn last night. She faced the window, eyes wide open and fixed. Sean sighed. He leaned up on his elbow and looked closer. That distant gaze. He reached his hand toward her cheek, then pulled back as he replayed that shrill scream deep in his mind. He felt so awful about what he had done to her last night. He still wasn't sure what it was, but he felt plenty awful.

She winked. "Gotcha, baby." She gripped Sean's hand and eased it up her skirt, then down her panties. He slid one finger inside her and she said, "That's nice. It's been too long." He massaged her clit. She suddenly pulled his hand out and jumped from the bed. She raced down the stairs like a kid closing on Christmas presents. Sean put on his sweatpants. His hard rod formed a tent at the front, and he decided he'd best wait for it to soften.

"Get your ass in gear, Sean! You gonna sleep the day away?"

He descended the stairs and followed an ant-crumb trail of

clothes: one shoe on the bedroom floor, one in the hall, blazer on the top stair, skirt midway down, blouse on the living room floor, slip draped on the cold TV, panty hose in front of the open back door.

Cathie skipped across the backyard like a young girl, her tousled hair flowing behind her. Her bra flew from her strong, lean shoulders and fell like matching parachutes halfway to the old tree. He froze on the porch. His heart raced as she gripped the trunk of the tree. His hard-on collapsed.

Cathie climbed. Sean's limbs tingled as she ascended higher into the dense leaves on one healthy side. She pulled off her panties and let them fall to the ground. Her pale skin sparkled behind the softly dancing leaves. "C'mon, baby."

Sean swallowed hard and walked to the trunk of the tree. Cathie had positioned herself up above a spot where the trunk split into two, her nude body stretched long.

There was a rustling in the yard next door. He whispered hoarsely, "Come down from there, Cathie."

"Make me." She opened her legs wide and suspended her body with her strong hands like a pole dancer. Her pussy lips were beautiful. Her pubic hair glistened.

He so wanted her, and his cock rose again. "Really, Cathie, this isn't funny."

"You were right, it's still a good, strong tree, see? Let's enjoy it."

Sean shook his head.

"Come on up. Please." She brought her legs back down and blew him a kiss.

All the worries, all the fears knotted in his stomach, while his desire to atone for the prior night emerged. He grabbed the trunk of the tree. He ascended through the inevitable woozy feeling. He started to tilt his head down.

"Eyes on me!" Cathie pointed to each spot he should grab as he climbed toward her.

He trembled when he finally stopped across from where Cathie was suspended. "Put your hands there and there." She directed him to lean back and grip two branches like a crucifixion. He did. Cathie leaned forward and took his jaw in her hands. "Thank you for being there for me last night." She yanked his sweatpants down and his cock sprung out like the sunrise. "Sorry I walked away. I hate to cry, just fucking hate it." Cathie straddled him and gripped around his shoulders. He was her only support, her legs dangled free, her pussy devoured him. "You feel so good in me." She kissed his neck, then bit one earlobe.

Brappa. Brappa. BZZZZZ!

Cathie arched her hips above Sean to expose almost every inch of his cock to the morning air, then she compressed tight again.

KHHRRRT!

She stared into his eyes as she fucked him with a perfect rhythm that only she knew. He was unspeakably excited and devoutly scared. The cocktail was heady. He wanted to come, but that would not be practical. "Please, ease up, Cathie."

The bark and spindles hurt. His fingers ached from holding the combined weights of their bodies writhing high in the balding tree. The echoes of the churning chainsaw and woodchips scattering in the next lawn could not overshadow the soft sound of Cathie's ascending breaths in his ear. "I want it. Let it go." She'd never asked verbally. Something in this struck him deeply and it took all his control not to release. He tried to distract himself, but it wasn't easy, poised in a tree, the nude body of his wife pounding his hips like the back of a cleaver tenderizing tough meat.

She grunted into him with a shuddering, explosive, but nearly silent orgasm. He was still hard in her, still needing, still trying to distract himself. He began to ease his cock out. "Okay, let's go inside, Cathie."

"You are inside. Please stay." She forced the weight of her hips down again. She reached around his biceps and the branches to brace them both. She moaned in time with the pumping of her hips and forced him to stare into her pale blue eyes.

"Oh, oh, Cathie. I—I—you know how I lose it when I come."

"That I do."

Sean's balls were tight as an underripe peach. His hands twitched, his feet started to lose their grip. He tried to hold back. He looked away. He held. He held.

Her lip touched his ear. "Let go, Sean. I need it."

He exploded, and a shockwave consumed his body as the chainsaw continued to methodically section the downed limbs of the fallen healthy oak next door. He gasped, writhed and gave a deep, hopeful, elated yell as he shot deep into Cathie's body. His body was beyond his control. The most beautiful smile he'd ever seen in his life opened across Cathie's lips; her lean biceps felt like a bodybuilder's as she suspended the two.

The chainsaw idled. A strong voice called out. "Who's out there?"

Sean looked out through the defiant leaves toward the workman who squinted, trying to make out where the sound had come from. "Get back to work." Sean deliberately lowered his voice an octave. Cathie popped one hand to her mouth to silence a laugh and they teetered to that side. Sean grabbed the limbs and held Cathie and him fast. She coiled to him again. Their combined grips suspended them like they were a part of the tree.

The spindles and bark of the tree felt good.

* * *

Sean and Cathie sat on the lawn chairs on the back porch, each wearing a robe, their bare legs resting on the same little stool, feet entwined. They looked toward the balding tree in the fading evening light. Cathie rested her palm in Sean's hand. "I made a nice sale today. Old neighborhood, young couple."

"Seems you're settling in at Harkin."

"I just had to realize that I'm not a hard sell."

"No shit?"

She laughed. "No shit. Wanna risk climbing a predatory tree?"

"I don't know—"

"C'mon." Cathie rose from the chair and lifted the hem of her robe to expose her beautiful, bare ass. She gripped Sean's hand tight and towed him toward the tree.

Sean's heart pounded double time and he pulled against her. She continued unabated, and he followed in choppy, hesitant steps until his stride widened with inflating confidence.

He paused at the trunk of the tree and watched her climb so nimbly. She stripped her robe off and let it fall to the ground. "Come on, slowpoke."

He kept his eyes on Cathie as he climbed.

THE MITZVAH

Tiffany Reisz

Day One was the hardest. Watching her husband Zachary trying to pin the torn bit of black ribbon to his jacket with trembling hands nearly broke her. Grace walked over and took the ribbon from him. As she pinned it to his lapel, Zachary pressed his forehead to hers and whispered, "Thank you." She couldn't even speak; she only nodded and kissed him quick.

Taking his hand, she followed him out of his childhood bedroom. Feeling lost among Zachary's Jewish family, Grace decided that keeping her mouth shut and staying close to her husband would be her strategy for the day. Zachary's grief at his mother's unexpected death two days ago had been so acute that Grace hardly gave her own sorrow a thought. She'd loved Sara, Zachary's mother, and still couldn't believe the beautiful woman who'd given her husband his ice-blue eyes and his black hair and his love of literature was gone. Sara had been the first of Zachary's family to embrace her after their suspiciously quick wedding seven years ago. "You're too young for him. And you're a gentile. But I know my son. He married you for love. Don't ever think otherwise."

Mute with grief, the Easton family assembled in the living room and filed out of the house and into cars. Grace glanced around at the other women and checked her dress against theirs. The youngest wife present by at least ten years, Grace feared her plain navy dress appeared too chic, too short. But her sister-in-law Dita, wife of Zachary's rabbi brother, wore a tailored black suit that showed off her shapely knees and calves. Dita caught Grace looking at her and smiled a reassurance. Grace smiled her gratitude back and slipped into the backseat of the car next to Zachary.

Alone with each other in the back of the car, Zachary squeezed her knee.

"How's my shiksa?" he asked, and Grace laughed a little.

"Your shiksa's okay. How are you?" she asked before she could stop herself. "Sorry. Terrible question."

Zachary gave her a tight smile. "You're here. I'll be fine. I think."

She clung to his hand. "I'm always here."

Grace looked away and gave him a moment's privacy to wipe the tear from his cheek.

Zachary, as a former literature professor and current editor of fiction, had been the natural choice to write and give the eulogy for the family matriarch. Grace thought she'd never survive those few hours yesterday when Zachary had holed up in his home office to write his final words to his mother. It took everything Grace had not to barge in and throw her arms around her husband and sob with him all night long. His grief came first, so she held it together, gave him his time alone and cried silently in their bed.

She closed her eyes and remembered last night. At one in the morning, Zachary had finally come to bed. She'd heard a noise and turned toward the sound. Watching her husband undress in the dark, she'd chided herself for thinking torrid thoughts of him even in their shared grief. He'd crawled across the sheets to her and pulled her small frame against his much larger, six-foot-tall self.

"We can't make love during shivah," he'd whispered in the dark.

"When does shivah start?" she'd asked, wrapping her arms around his muscular shoulders.

"Tomorrow. After the funeral."

"How long does it last?"

Zachary kissed her lips. She could feel the tension in his taut body as she ran her hands up and down his arms.

"Seven days," he breathed.

"Oh, god," she said. Zachary had laughed softly—the first laugh she'd heard from him since yesterday—as he pushed her gently onto her back.

He slipped his hand into her pajama pants and pushed a finger into her. Part of her relished the pleasure of reconnecting with him after so many hours of separation. But a small voice in her head told her she should be grieving right now, not panting underneath her husband.

"Are you sure?"

"Please, Gracie. I need this," he'd whispered, and she'd slipped out of her clothes and opened her legs wide for him. He teased her clitoris with his fingertips and gently sucked on her nipples until they hardened in his warm mouth. Even in his sadness, he would never take her until her body was wet and ready.

When he entered her, she'd wrapped her legs around his lower back and clung to him with all her strength and all her love.

Missionary wasn't one of their favorite positions. Zachary far preferred her on her stomach, his hand in her long red hair, and with his chest to her back and his mouth to her ear. But tonight she felt he needed to make love to her face-to-face, needed the comfort of her whole body wrapped around him.

As he thrust into her, she caressed his strong back with her hands and his shoulder with her lips. Exhausted from grief and stress and packing for their week ahead at his parents' house, Grace couldn't relax enough to come. It didn't matter. This time was for Zachary and she whispered that into his ear.

"Are you sure?" He kissed her face, her neck.

"Yes. Just come when you need to. Use me." She rocked her hips in that way that always made his breath catch. "I want you to."

He nodded and dug his hands into the soft skin of her thighs and thrust harder. Grace lay beneath him, happy she could do this one small thing to comfort him. He came with a quiet shudder and lingered inside her for a few minutes more before pulling out.

"One week," she repeated. "Whoever invented shivah must be a sadist." Grace ran her fingers over her husband's handsome features. She loved his forehead the most. Or maybe his strong nose. His sculpted lips had given her more than a few happy memories.

"I think God invented shivah," Zachary answered, pulling her to him and resting his head on her shoulder.

Grace rolled onto her other side and pressed her back to Zachary's chest. He held her tight to him and she felt a tear sliding down her face. She couldn't be sure if the tear belonged to her or him.

"I stand by my words."

Finally at the funeral home, Grace refused to let go of Zachary's hand. The few hugs he gave, he gave one-armed, while his other arm stayed with her. They took their seats in the front rows as Zachary's brother, Rabbi Aaron Easton, led them in prayers. Usually she loved seeing him in his yarmulke. She found the traditional head-covering quite adorable. But today he looked grim and somber. Grace tensed as the time arrived for Zachary to read his eulogy.

His brother called him forward and Zachary squeezed her hand once, released it and walked to the front. He pulled his notes from his jacket pocket and opened his mouth. Nothing came out. Grace's stomach dropped. Zachary took a deep breath and his brother reached out and touched his arm. Grace didn't know what to do. She wanted to sob, to grab Zachary and sink to the floor with him and wail. Instead she stood up calmly and walked to him. She twined her arm through his, took his notes and began to read.

"My mother," Grace began, wanting to cry but laughing instead as she read out loud the words of her husband's eulogy, "would threaten to slap us all if she saw us right now. And then she'd make us eat something."

That night Grace lay next to Zachary in his childhood bed at his parents' home and reminded herself that it was only Day One of Shivah. And they had six days left to get through before she and Zachary could make love again. She knew it would make the waiting so much harder if she touched him, but she couldn't stop herself from draping herself over his chest and pressing her ear to him.

"Your heart's still beating," Grace said as Zachary laid his arm over her back.

"That's a comfort."

"It is. It's never allowed to stop beating."

"It stopped once," Zachary said, tracing her shoulder blade with his fingertips.

Grace looked up at him. "When?"

"The day I met you."

Grace said nothing. She just crawled up his body and kissed him long and deep. Zachary took her face in his hands and didn't let her move away for a solid five minutes.

With a shuddering breath, Grace pulled away from her husband and lay on her side away from him.

He lay close and rubbed her feet with his until she giggled.

"Not quite as good as sex, but footsie will tide me over," she said, play-kicking him.

"She wouldn't care, you know." Zachary slipped his hand under her shirt and touched her back.

"But you do care. Even if you won't admit it."

Zachary sighed. "I do. I don't know why I do, but I do. I'm usually a terrible Jew." Grace laughed.

"Well, considering I'm Welsh Presbyterian, I really don't think I can judge how good of a Jew you are or not. But you did worship your mother so I hear that makes you quite a good Jewish boy. And she died three days ago. So I think she and I both would understand if your mind were on something other than sex with your wife."

"It's a novel sensation."

"What is?"

"Having my mind be on something other than sex with my wife," Zachary said, moving closer to her but making no move to undress her. "Not sure I like it."

Day Two had gone a little better. A steady stream of friends and relatives, many of whom she'd never met before, kept her mind off her grief. But by Day Three, Grace woke up dreading another night lying next to her husband and feeling guilty about how desperately she wanted to climb onto him, take him inside her, and help him forget all his pain, if only for an hour or two.

On Day Four, Grace had had enough of the house of grief. She pulled on her trainers and went for an early morning run before the parade of friends and relatives started again. When she made it back to the house, wet with sweat and shivering from cold, she found her sister-in-law Dita in the kitchen.

"Tea?" Dita offered, and Grace accepted with gratitude. "How are you holding up? It must be strange for you. Zachary tells me this is your first Jewish funeral."

Grace sipped at her tea.

"It's different. I appreciate the rituals—covering the mirrors, not cooking, not going out. It's just...difficult. And more than a little frustrating."

"Yes, I miss the sex, too."

Grace's eyes went wide. Then she covered her mouth to stifle an unruly laugh.

"Dita, I didn't say—"

"You didn't have to," Dita said, pouring milk into her black tea. "It's nice to see that after seven years, you and Zachary still can't keep your eyes off of each other. You might love him as much as I love Aaron. Maybe."

"A close second at least. Yes. I'm not a fan of that particular provision of shivah. But Zachary's really grieving. I'm sure it's for the best."

Dita rolled her eyes. "Nonsense. He needs his wife. And he needs a distraction. You can be both."

"Not for three more days," Grace said and counted not just the days but the hours until she and Zachary would be free of shivah and back home in their bedroom in London again.

"I'll tell you a little secret from a Jew to a shiksa," Dita said, leaning in. "Life comes before death. When a funeral procession meets a wedding procession, the wedding procession goes first. Shivah's suspended during shabbat, Grace. And the shabbat starts at sundown tonight. And...during shabbat, sex with your spouse is a mitzvah." A mitzvah, Grace knew, was a good deed, a divine commandment.

"Dita, I'm ready to convert."

"Don't you dare. I love having a redheaded shiksa for a sister-in-law."

Grace took Dita's advice to heart. She said nothing to Zachary, merely watched him all day looking for any signs that any advances on her part would be unwelcome that night. But as they sat side by side greeting yet another stream of visitors, Zachary rarely stopped touching her. He'd rest his hand on her knee or lightly scratch her back. His grief today seemed heart-rending as usual, but calmer now. Late in the afternoon, the house emptied and the Easton family started to get ready for shul.

"Would I be a horrible wife if I didn't go with you?" Grace asked.

"I'd consider it grounds for divorce," Zachary deadpanned. "No, of course you don't have to go. Go out. Eat something very un-kosher for me. Please."

"I'll have a bacon sandwich in your honor," Grace said, kissing him. "I'll see you later."

Food wasn't on Grace's mind—just her handsome husband and how she would go about comforting him that night. The usual fare, although fantastically enjoyable for the both of them, might not provide the distraction he needed.

Once alone in the house, Grace stood in Zachary's childhood bedroom and looked around. She smiled at the photos of him in his footballer's uniform. At thirty-eight, Zachary remained as handsome as he was twenty years ago when the pictures were taken. More handsome even, as time had turned him from a sweet-faced if rather rakish youth into the more chiseled, masculine adult he'd become. Sometimes she still couldn't believe they'd made it seven years. They married under horrible circumstances—the one-night indiscretion between teacher and student, the pregnancy, losing the baby only a few weeks into their tenuous marriage. They'd done everything wrong in the beginning so that it amazed her how right it had turned out.

The picture of him playing football with his friends gave her a delicious idea. She dug through his closet, through his old clothes his mother had kept in perfect condition, until she found his old Everton football jersey. A quick run to the shop on the corner provided the other two items she'd need for the night. By late evening, she lounged on his bed, eager for him to return home.

She heard voices in the entryway and felt a sudden surge of nervousness. Grace had never seduced her husband before. When it came to Zachary, seduction was a moot point. She couldn't remember a time when he hadn't been in the mood. Seducing Zachary required nothing more than showing up.

But never before had he been in deep mourning. A small part of her feared he'd turn her down and accuse her of insensitivity. Grace had halfway convinced herself to throw on her clothes before he came upstairs. But then she heard footsteps outside the door.

Grace lay on her back and propped her legs up on the wall. Her head draped off the edge of the bed so when Zachary entered and saw her, she at first thought he was frowning.

"Gracie? Is that my old football jersey?"

"Why do they call football soccer in America?" Grace asked, crossing her legs at the ankles. She'd bought some boys' tube socks at the corner shop with blue stripes on them. In addition to the socks and the jersey, she wore the laciest pair of knickers she'd packed and nothing else.

"I knew before I opened the door. Now suddenly, I seem to have forgotten."

Zachary closed the door and walked over to the bed.

"I'll teach you something," Grace said as Zachary sat next to her and ran his hand up and down her bare thighs. "Dita told me that on Shabbat, it's a mitzvah to have sex with your spouse. Even during shivah."

"You're starting to sound like a Jew, Gracie."

"L'Chaim."

Zachary bent to kiss her lips but Grace rolled away from him at the last second. She came up on her hands and knees and threw her full weight into knocking him onto his back.

"You don't get to kiss me yet," she said. "I get to kiss you. You just lie there and behave yourself."

"I can promise to lie here until you tell me otherwise. The 'behaving myself' ceased to be an option when you put on those clothes."

"Like it?" Grace straddled his hips and smiled down at him. She ran her hands down her stomach and started to lift the jersey up. But before she bared her breasts, she pulled it back down again and gave him a wicked smile.

Grace started unbuttoning his shirt. She went slowly, one button at a time, and dropped a kiss on his chest and stomach as she revealed more and more of her husband's lean, muscular body.

She didn't stop with his shirt. She unbuttoned his pants and freed his erection. Running her hand up and down his hard length, she grinned at him.

"This, I've missed." Grace teased the tip before wrapping her entire hand around him.

"This has missed you, too." Zachary inhaled sharply.

"Have you missed your wife sucking your cock?" Grace

asked as she flicked her tongue over him.

"Grace," Zachary breathed, half laughing. "What's gotten into you?"

Grace grinned at him. Dirty talk in bed was Zachary's forte, not hers. He'd often whisper his lecherous intentions to her during foreplay while she panted and blushed. This might have been the first time she'd ever said "cock" in their seven years of marriage.

"You've gotten into me. See?"

Grace put him in her mouth and sucked hard and deep.

Zachary gripped the sheets as his hips lifted off the bed. She massaged his full length with her lips and plied him over and over again with her tongue. His breaths came hard and fast so Grace stopped and pulled up.

"Not so fast. No coming without me."

"A fair rule," Zachary said, his voice hoarse with need.

Grace took a deep breath and rolled onto her back. Zachary sat up next to her.

"I await your orders," he said.

"Your order," Grace said, as she slid her knickers down her legs, "is to do nothing but watch."

Trying to hide her nervousness, Grace opened her thighs and hooked her knee around Zachary's back. She slipped her hand between her legs, spread herself open and started playing with her clitoris.

"God, Gracie," Zachary said, digging his fingers into her calf. He loved watching her masturbate. And she loved pleasing him. But doing this in front of him, even after so many years together, still mortified her. Zachary's chest heaved and the sight of him so aroused goaded her on. Her clitoris swelled against her fingers and she felt herself growing wetter.

"Zachary," Grace said as she slid a finger into herself and

smiled as Zachary's eyes went wide at the sight. After seven years, it did her heart good to know she could still shock him. "I think I need to fuck you. If you don't mind."

"I won't object to it."

Zachary started to crawl onto her but she stopped him with a hand on his chest. "On your back. My turn to be on top," she said. Maybe once a month Grace would work up the courage to straddle him and take him inside her. She loved the angle of penetration in that position but felt so exposed kneeling naked on top of him.

"I've heard of women like you," Zachary said, amused suspicion in his voice. "Are you a dominatrix?"

"I'm a horny wife who wants her husband inside her. Do you mind?"

"Not a bit."

Zachary obediently lay on his back and Grace started to straddle his stomach. At the last moment she changed her mind and turned her back to him. She'd read in some women's magazine about the position called reverse cowgirl. Ridiculous name but apparently men loved the view. Grace faced Zachary's feet and took him in her hand again. She rose up, positioned him at the wet entrance of her body and sunk down onto him.

Sighing with bliss, Grace took all of him into her.

"Have I ever told you how much I love feeling your cock in me?" Grace asked.

"Not in so many words," Zachary said, his voice breaking as she started rocking her hips.

"It's the best feeling in the world. I feel complete when you're inside me, thrusting into me." Grace reached down and gently cupped his testicles while she moved her hips in tight spirals. They'd never done this position before but Grace decided they might need to add it to their repertoire after tonight. Zachary panted underneath her. Now she understood why he preferred being on top during lovemaking. The power she felt to make him gasp as she inflicted pleasure on him was well worth any embarrassment.

Grace leaned forward and put her full weight onto her hands in front of her. She rocked her hips back and forth faster. Zachary grabbed her hips and pulled her down hard onto him.

Fearing the thin walls, Grace came hard but quietly as Zachary thrust up and into her. Still inside her, he rolled up and wrapped his arms around her and slipped his hands under her jersey.

"What are you doing?" Grace demanded as she slowly caught her breath.

"Touching your nipples," Zachary said. "Is that not allowed?"

"Your cock's in me and I'm wet with your come. Anything's allowed at this point."

"I have to say this scandalous talk of yours comes as quite a shock, Mrs. Easton."

"Aren't you the one who said last weekend that you wanted to, and I quote, 'Fuck me until I forgot my name, fuck me until I couldn't walk and fuck me until your come dripped down my legs?'"

"I said that?"

"You did. You were fucking me at the time. And I believe this may be the most I've ever said 'fuck' in my life."

"I'm very proud of you, Gracie. Is there anything else you want to say to me? Or do to me? Or have me do to you?"

"You can kiss my clit until I come again. Just a suggestion."

"Would I be allowed to suck your nipples first and put two fingers inside you?"

"No."

"No?"

"I want three fingers. At least."

Grace laughed as Zachary collapsed onto his back in a pretend faint. At moments like this she knew with crystal clarity why their marriage had worked against all odds. The sex didn't keep them together. The laughter did.

Slowly Grace crawled off Zachary and lay on her back again.

"Forgive me, Grace, but I'm afraid I may have to reposition you."

"Do whatever you feel is best."

Grace let out a shocked laugh as Zachary sank onto his knees on the floor by the bed, grabbed her and yanked her hips to the edge of the mattress. His childhood bed sat low enough to the ground that her very tall husband could spread her legs, lean over her body, lift her jersey, and take a nipple into his mouth.

"My wife has the most perfect breasts," he noted, and Grace grinned.

"Your wife's breasts are freckled."

"The freckles are my favorite part."

Zachary continued to sensually torture her breasts with his lips and tongue. He kissed his way down her stomach as he pinched and rolled her nipples between his dexterous fingers.

When they married, Zachary had slept with at least fifty women. But she never experienced much jealousy when she thought of his past lovers. They'd taught him well and now she reaped the benefits. Zachary's head pressed between her open thighs and he took her clitoris between his lips.

"Do you like tasting yourself in me?" Grace asked as Zachary's tongue pushed inside her. "I've always wondered that."

"Very much," Zachary said as he pulled his mouth from her and slipped two fingers into her. "I suppose it's a caveman male possessive instinct. It's my semen inside you and no one else's."

"Your semen, your cock, your tongue, your fingers...no one but you ever."

"You're welcome to tattoo that on your inner thigh."

"It's written on my heart." Grace came up on her elbows to meet his eyes. "Good enough?"

Zachary didn't answer at first. He reached out and cupped her face with his hand. "It's perfect."

Grace's heart fluttered.

"I love you, Professor Easton," Grace whispered.

"I love you, Mrs. Easton," Zachary answered. "Now lie back. I've only got two fingers in you and I believe you demanded three."

"At least," she reminded him.

Grace relaxed onto her back and stared at the ceiling as her husband opened her wider. They'd never done anything more than three fingers on occasion. Slim and small-boned, Grace's body was naturally tight; in the beginning, it took a couple of weeks with a very patient Zachary before she could have completely pain-free intercourse. But tonight she felt wild and wanton and wanted to try everything they hadn't done before.

Zachary spread his fingers apart inside her and Grace whimpered with the flash of pleasure mixed with pain.

"You know what would really help here?" Zachary asked. "Lube. Wish we'd packed it."

Grace slipped her hand under the pillow.

"Here. Bought it tonight. I mortified the poor teenage clerk. I suppose he can't imagine what an old married woman needed with lubricant and boys' tube socks."

"You're twenty-six and stunning. He'll probably masturbate every time he sees a pair of tube socks for the rest of his life."

As Grace laughed, Zachary applied the lubricant to her

vagina. Suddenly three fingers fit inside her perfectly.

"That's amazing," Grace moaned, her back arching.

"Does it hurt at all?"

"None. Can we try another?"

"You are insatiable tonight, aren't you?"

"You can't imagine how much I've missed you inside me this week. I respect shivah. I do. And I've felt so guilty. You're grieving and I am, too, but I lie next to you and think about how much I want you to make love to me."

"You should never feel guilty about wanting me to make love to you. I don't care if I'm on my deathbed and the world is burning down. Understood?"

Grace smiled at the ceiling.

"Understood."

Zachary opened her up more as his fingers probed inside her. She flinched as his knuckles grazed her G-spot, gasped as he went deep enough that she felt his fingertip against her cervix. He pushed a fourth finger into her, as his thumb made tight circles on her clitoris. Grace's heart raced. Her inner muscles tightened. She came hard around his hand buried deep inside her.

"Grace, I have to fuck you," Zachary said. "Please."

"Fuck me till I forget my name," she said. "And yours. Whoever you are."

Laughing, Zachary stood up and put his knee on the bed beside her hip. He started to push inside her.

"Wait. Not like that," she said, stopping him.

"How then? I will stand on my head and fuck you if you want me to."

Grace reached down and found the lube again. She held it up and stared into her husband's eyes without saying a word.

"Are you sure, Gracie?"

They'd never done anal before. Zachary had done it, of

course, but Grace had never worked up the nerve to try it with him. She knew he wanted to. There wasn't much in the bedroom that Zachary didn't want to do. But tonight she wanted to show him with her body how much she loved him. This seemed the perfect time to try.

"Yes."

Zachary nodded and pulled his shirt off as Grace rolled over onto her stomach.

She breathed slowly and listened as Zachary finished undressing completely.

"Don't tense," Zachary warned, as he slipped two wet fingers into her. "Relax and tell me if it hurts."

Grace nodded and closed her eyes. She felt Zachary at the tight entrance of her body. He pressed in slowly, thrusting gently. Zachary's fingers gripped the sheets by her face. Grace reached out and wrapped her hand around his thumb. Groaning softly, he twined his hand into hers and pushed in a little harder.

"Please stop me if you want to," Zachary said and Grace could hear the hunger in his voice, the desire to never stop.

"No. It feels strange. But I do like it."

Zachary slipped his other hand under the jersey she still wore and caressed her back as he moved in her. She did like this new unusual way he filled her. And she felt so wicked lying on her stomach, her sock-clad feet hanging in the air. But the best part was Zachary, the way he breathed so hard, how desperately he held her hand. He thrust a few more times and came inside her with a throaty gasp.

Carefully, he pulled out of her. She tossed him her knickers and he used them to clean the lubricant off. Now completely naked, Zachary stretched out on top of her and kissed her mouth, teased her lips with his tongue, and held her so tightly to him she could scarcely breathe.

Grace started to say something but a soft banging sound from the next room down interrupted her. A bang followed by a moan. Zachary's eyes brightened with quiet laughter.

"What is that?" Grace asked.

"Aaron and Dita." Zachary slipped his hand under her jersey to cup her breast. "She's rather enthusiastic, isn't she?"

"If we can hear them, does that mean they heard us?" Grace asked, flushing with embarrassment.

"After your last orgasm? I'm absolutely sure of it."

"Oh, god. Your brother's a rabbi," she reminded him.

"Don't worry. Remember," Zachary said, pushing her legs open with his knees. "It's Shabbat and we're married. This is a mitzvah."

AFTER THE MASSAGE

Kay Jaybee

F licking a stray lock of red hair out of the way, Jess pushed
her mobile harder against her ear as she marched along the
high street. Her heart thudded against her chest as she waited
for Lee to answer. At last Jess heard a muffled click, telling her
he'd put his phone on hands-free listening. Without giving him
the chance to speak, she blurted, "Where are you?"

"About seven miles from town. Why?"

"Well, I need you at my place. Now!" Jess kept her voice
low as she weaved her way along the busy street. "I need your
hands, your mouth and your cock."

"Fuck, woman, I'm driving!"

"Then drive faster, I'm horny as hell here."

Lee couldn't help but laugh. "What's got into you?"

"I just had a massage."

"So? Frank's always giving you a massage."

Jess stopped marching, and, sheltered in a secluded shop
doorway, trying to calm her racing pulse, replied, "It wasn't

Frank. He's got a new assistant, Ali. Oh hell, Lee…"

Lee eased his foot off the accelerator; suddenly Jess had his undivided attention. "A male Ali, or a female Ali?"

"You should have seen her. Hot or what!"

Checking his transit's mirrors, Lee increased his speed, and overtook everything he safely could, making a beeline for Jess. "A hot woman?"

"I knew you'd like that." Jess licked her dry lips as she recalled the unexpectedly eventful hour she'd just spent. "I sure did."

Jess smiled to herself as she began to walk again, taking the most direct route home. She could hear the new husky edge to Lee's words as he asked the inevitable question. "What did she look like?"

"Petite, blonde, large blue eyes with long lashes, and I swear she was one hell of a flirt."

"Did you flirt back?"

"What do you think?"

"Of course you did, don't know why I even asked, you're such a dirty bitch."

"This is true." Jess gripped the mobile tighter. "I'm nearly home; where are you now?"

"About five miles away, and thanks to you, I'm as stiff as a board."

"Good. You get yourself here, and I'll give that cock what it so badly wants."

"I won't have long, babe, so make sure you're waiting good and naked."

Jess switched off the phone and broke into a jog. A few moments later she was outside her home, shrugging off her coat as she unlocked the door, abandoning her boots in an untidy pile on the hall floor. As she walked into the living room, Jess began to deposit her clothing, dropping her skirt, shirt and underwear like a trail of breadcrumbs for Lee to follow when he arrived.

Naked, as per her lover's request, Jess sat on the cream leather sofa, enjoying the caress of its cool fabric against her flesh. Flushed from the effort of her run, the aftermath of her massage and the thought of what would happen once Lee got there, Jess closed her eyes and leaned back against the seat. In her mind she could clearly see Ali, her long manipulating fingers topped with neat purple nails, her lash-veiled eyes wide open, her whole body exuding confidence. She must have been at least five years younger than Jess, maybe about twenty-six, but Ali was undoubtedly an expert in her profession and a born tease.

Flirting was second nature to Jess; she did it all the time. Usually it was playfully received as the innocent fun it was, but that morning had been different and she knew it. Jess had received upper back and neck massages from both male and female masseurs every month for years; she knew exactly how they were supposed to make her feel. Today's experience, as she'd lain semi-naked on the soft massage bench, had been totally at odds with the usual sensation of muscular stupor. For one thing, Ali's manipulations had not kept to the flat of her back or the roll of her shoulders.

The first time an individual fingertip had strayed down her side and briefly brushed the edge of her left breast, Jess had been surprised but had just assumed the girl was inexperienced and had made an innocent mistake.

When it happened a second time, however, and the single digit was joined by another that ran the entire length of her squashed tits, making her body tense automatically against the table, Jess knew she had entered unexpected territory. She'd been about to say something, when Ali had moved her hands away again and begun to professionally pummel Jess's knotted shoulders.

Jess sighed as she remembered, allowing her own fingers to

slide across her breasts. Where the hell was Lee? She couldn't wait any longer for him to arrive, for not only was she desperate to feel his dick between her legs, she was dying to see the look on his face when she told him about the final and most interesting part of her massage.

Her palms began to slip lingeringly down her body. With eyes still closed, Jess continued to pretend they belonged to Ali, tracing the outline of her chest.

When she heard the front door swing open and then hastily slam shut, Jess moved one hand to her pussy, rubbing at her wet clit. Her arousal increased at the thought of the picture she must be creating for her partner, as he walked through the door and saw her wanking off.

Lee's groan echoed around the room as he stood before Jess, his deep, dark eyes wide as he watched her writhe against the sofa. With her head thrown back against the cushions and her legs stretched open, Jess was a picture of wanton lust. He ripped his clothes from his body, his thick cock springing toward her, pointing at Jess accusingly.

Jess's eyes snapped open, and she smiled with mischief as she leaned forward, watching him intently as he rolled a condom onto his delicious length. Then, grabbing at his tanned body, she dragged Lee down next to her, before jumping across his legs and impaling herself on his rigid length with a relieved whine, ruffling the warm hairs that were sprinkled across the top of his toned chest.

"Tell me about her," Lee spoke urgently into Jess's shoulder as she pumped against his shaft, "Tell me! I don't have long."

Speaking in a breathless whisper, Jess muttered into his ear as she continued to glide up and down his shaft. "At first I thought Ali was touching my tits by mistake, but she *soooo* wasn't." Jess felt Lee's body tense further beneath her words as she continued. "Her hands were so warm, so firm. She told me my tits were beautiful; she told me she'd wanted to touch them from the moment I'd walked into her room, and that somehow she'd known I wouldn't object."

Lee's voice was barely audible as he spoke. "What did you do?"

"Nothing, I just let her 'accidentally' touch me, and 'accidentally' roll me onto my back so she could massage my front as well as my shoulders." Jess paused, her voice catching in her throat as Lee dipped a finger over her clit, circling over and around it with expert precision.

"Did you fuck?"

"No." Jess felt her legs began to quiver and her stomach flutter, as Lee thrust back against her, increasing their combined rhythm. "I told her about your deepest, darkest fantasy."

"No way!"

"Oh, yes way." Jess's reply turned into a breathless whisper as she started to come against his dick.

"Go baby! Come around my cock!" Temporarily distracted from Jess's story, Lee moved faster still, his eyes creased in pleasure. "I'm coming, too, babe," he said through clenched teeth as he fiercely spunked into her.

The moment their bodies stilled, Lee stared at Jess's chest, his expression still hungry for information. "So, she liked these, did she?"

"She did." Jess shuffled closer to him, her body still hypersensitive from her climax as she enjoyed the tickle of his chest hairs against her breasts.

"What did she say when you told her about my fantasy?"

"She asked me about you, what you look like, what you do for a living and stuff, and then she told me her fantasy in return."

"And?" Lee worked his calloused touch over her tits, making it impossible for Jess to reply for a while. Then, panting out her words, she finally said, "We agreed to combine her fantasy and yours."

"What do you mean?" Lee flicked Jess's right nipple hard, and then, moving down to her pussy, he brought Jess quickly to a shuddering second orgasm.

Jess lay back, wallowing in the feelings of lingering stimulation and satisfaction that rippled across her body. She watched Lee start to dress, and then weighed in with the punchline to her story. "Ali said she would let you watch her fuck me, as per your fantasy, if we can do it in your van, as per her fantasy."

Lee froze in the act of pulling his dirty gray T-shirt over his head. "She said what?"

"You heard me." Jess looked up at him through her eyelashes. "So, what do you think?"

"She really is up for it?" Lee sat back down next to the incredible creature on the sofa.

"Yes."

"And you'd really do it? You'd really have sex with a woman so I could watch?" Lee regarded Jess with hopeful disbelief.

"Sure. It's not like it would be the first time, honey." Jess grinned lazily as she stroked his stubbled chin. "And anyway, I'd pretty much do anything for you, you know that."

Lee stared hard at Jess. "My van?"

"Yes, Ali has a thing about tradesmen, apparently. You should have seen her face when I told her you were a plumber; something about tool belts and men who are ready for anything, I think."

Struggling to bring himself back to reality, Lee glanced at his watch. "I've really got to go, I'm late already."

Jess nodded. "You think about it while you work."

Lee shook his head, amazement etched on his face, "Think about it! I'm gonna have a hard-on all bloody day!"

He had parked his van in a deserted lay-by along a quiet country road. Lee could almost hear how fast the adrenaline was pumping through his body. The idea of watching Jess with another woman had been the stuff of his wanking fantasies ever since she'd blown him away with her confession of bisexuality six months ago. Now, as he waited for Jess to bring Ali to the same location, the back of Lee's neck prickled with excitement, his imagination surging ahead to all the things he hoped he was about to witness.

The crunch of car tires drawing up behind the van alerted him to the arrival of the women. Suddenly he was unsure of himself. *Should he leap out of his seat and greet them? Should he wait to be invited?*

He'd spent an hour that afternoon clearing out the usual contents of his van, so that the three of them would have room to move. He'd left the narrow shelves full of tools, which were fixed high up on the walls, hoping they wouldn't be in the way, but he'd covered the dirty floor with travel blankets, and placed three battery-powered lanterns along one side of the van, so he would have some light to watch the forthcoming show by.

The van rocked as the back doors were opened and Lee felt someone—no, two people—climb into the back. He gripped the steering wheel and took a long deep breath. This was it. Lee could feel his dick poking hard beneath his jeans, fighting to break free from the navy boxers that held it in place.

Were they naked already? Was Jess running her tongue over this unknown woman's breasts? Lee jumped down from his seat and raced to the back of the van. Pulling the doors open wide, he was greeted by a sight that would stay with him for the rest of his life.

Dressed only in matching black bras and knickers, they sat cross-legged in front of each other on the dusty rugs, their pale outlines illuminated by the glow of his lamps.

"Come on, then." Jess beckoned Lee to approach, a devastatingly wicked grin lighting up her stunning green eyes.

Lee's gaze rested on the other woman—Ali, he presumed—as he jumped into his van and closed the double doors behind him. Shadows clouded his vision as he became accustomed to the dim light.

Jess pointed to the far end of the vehicle, and Lee obediently went and sat down. Despite the van's large capacity, he felt incredibly uncomfortable as he crouched in the confined space, his dick harder than ever before, squashed between his trousers and cramped legs.

His discomfort, however, was soon forgotten as their small blonde guest moved closer to Jess, reaching her arms out and unclipping Jess's satin bra, releasing her tits for them all to see. Lee wasn't sure if it was he or Ali who gave the loudest sigh in appreciation of their creamy beauty.

Lee's throat, already dry with anticipation, sealed shut as Ali wasted no time in attaching her red lips to his lover's right tit, making Jess close her eyes and tilt her head back in delicious response.

Shuffling a little closer, Lee rocked onto his knees. No way could he leave his cock trapped where it was. Hastily, he fumbled at his belt and was soon groaning in relief as his shaft sprang free, his grip closing around its length, his eyes never leaving the two women.

Jess, a look of complete bliss on her face, had totally surrendered herself to the other woman's caresses. Ali's hands were everywhere at once—Jess's chest, stomach, arms and hair. As Lee watched, almost hypnotized by the erotic tableau, her mouth came to Jess's for the first time.

Sweat began to gather on Lee's forehead, and the air in the van suddenly felt unbearably muggy as the women attacked each other's lips with an almost savage hunger. Jess, her temporary submissiveness forgotten, unhooked Ali's bra as they kissed, kneading the small neat breasts, making Ali squeak approvingly into Jess's mouth.

Unable to content himself with just holding his swollen cock, Lee began to jerk it slowly against his fist. He really wanted to last until the girls were done, but they were just so hot, and shit, now they were running their fingers around the lacy edging of each other's knickers. As Ali inched down Jess's underwear, revealing the familiar small triangle of pussy hair he knew so well, Lee moaned softly. He wasn't even aware he'd been holding his breath as Jess removed Ali's briefs, and he let out a long jolting gasp at the sight of her clean-shaven mound.

There was a moment's total silence then, as the women, both standing, their heads brushing the van's ceiling, regarded each other, their chests heaving. Lee's hand stilled on his shaft as, with a lump in his throat, he waited.

Ali's eyes strayed from her temporary companion to the shelves of plumbing equipment Lee had left in the van. Reaching past Jess, she picked up a length of blue rope and began to toy with it suggestively.

Lee's dick gave an involuntary leap as he watched Jess, usually so dominant, so in control, turn around and willingly place her wrists behind her back, allowing them to be tied without a murmur of complaint. He knew they must have discussed this, and devised a plan of action that took them way beyond his fantasy. Lee watched eagerly for Ali's next move.

She placed her palms on Jess's shoulders and pushed her to the floor. Very soon Jess was lying flat on her stomach, her arms uncomfortably fastened up behind her. She lifted her face slightly so she could look at Lee; her eyes were brimming with desire as she asked him, "Are you having a good time, honey?"

Lee could barely reply. His throat felt as though he'd just trekked the Sahara. He simply nodded emphatically, making Jess laugh at his voyeuristic pleasure. Her laugh, however, was short-lived as the expression on Lee's face changed dramatically. She didn't have the chance to turn to see what Lee had seen, as a burning red pain seared through her backside.

Lee watched, open-mouthed, as Ali threw her arm back again in the confined space and struck Jess hard on the rump with the strap of his tool belt.

His lover's face was blotched with agony, and tears oozed at the corners of her eyes, but he could see from her expression that she was enjoying every painful moment as Ali increased the pace of her chastisement.

As her pale butt turned from its usual peachy cream to crimson, Jess's cries became less urgent, and a guttural strangled whine took over as she got closer and closer to coming beneath the punishment. Unable to resist touching his partner any longer, Lee moved to her face and stroked Jess's sweat-soaked fringe from her eyes. Never had he seen such a picture of lust on her face. He knew she was dangerously close to climax as, with one final strike, Ali managed to aim a blow across both cheeks at the same time.

The second the frayed brown leather connected with Jess, Ali dropped her weapon. Then, kneeling behind the bruising ass, she began to tenderly kiss and lick the wounds she'd inflicted.

Lee whimpered in unison with Jess in the face of Ali's exquisite attention. Continuing to soothe the damaged skin, Ali slipped a digit between Jess's legs and, although Lee couldn't actually see what she was doing, from the reaction of Jess's exhausted body, he knew she was playing with Jess's soaking pussy and clit.

Jess began to shake, gently at first, and then more severely as Ali continued to aggravate her nub. Lee couldn't hold back any longer. Scrambling to his feet, he stood, stooping a little against the roof of the van, and began to yank himself off over Jess's prone and quivering body. It only took a few sharp tugs for a fountain of pent-up spunk to spray across her in an urgent hot wave.

Lee fell back against the side of the van, resting against the narrow shelf units. She'd done it. She'd actually allowed him to watch her with another woman. Jess was truly unbelievable.

The show wasn't quite over, though. Ali bent down and gently undid Jess's rope restraints, and with practiced hands, began to massage some life back into her client's shoulders. Then, without a word passing between them, Jess turned, and with great speed of movement, pushed Ali down onto her back, spread her legs wide and dropped between them with a hungry mouth.

Lee's eyes burned in the scene, not wanting to miss a single lick, as Jess brought Ali to a rewarding climax of her own.

"Will you see her again?" An hour later, Lee was lathering soap across Jess's back as the shower thundered down onto them.

"I don't think so." She turned and looked at her man through the cascade of steaming water. "Fantasies are supposed to be a one-off thing, after all."

"I think I'm in shock." Lee wiped some droplets from her face. "You really did do that for me, didn't you? It wasn't some sort of incredible dream?"

"It was no dream. And it was hardly a chore." Jess gently

scratched her fingernails over his hard torso. "The question is, will you act out a fantasy for me now?"

Lee beamed. "And that fantasy would be?"

"You'll just have to wait and see, won't you?"

PINK SATIN PURSE

Donna George Storey

Scene One: The Bedroom, Midafternoon

I'm finally going to do it. Tonight.

Natalie actually said the words out loud to the empty room. Although her voice was brave, her tongue suddenly felt shamefully heavy in her mouth, even tingling, provocatively, at the tip.

Nervous as she was, she couldn't pass up this perfect opportunity to translate her guilty fantasy into action. She and Keenan had a rare evening alone—their daughter off to the movies with friends, their son invited to a sleepover birthday party. Her husband would already be expecting special date-night sex, something a bit edgy with plenty of loud moaning. However, he probably wouldn't be expecting what she would propose they try tonight. Or rather what she would command him to do.

For that is how she always imagined the scene, beginning with her own disembodied voice ordering him gently, but firmly:

Get on your hands and knees. Good boy. Now spread your legs wider for me...

Natalie swallowed hard and walked over to her dresser. Hooking her fingers through the pulls of the second-to-the-top drawer, she eased it open. She still felt a pang of surprise at the neatly arranged display of "adult" playthings before her. A sex stash was supposed to be a riotous jumble of satin and silicone, but somehow she craved order here more than in other parts of her life. Her collection of thigh-highs—in classic black, bridal cream and Keenan's favorite whore's red—were tucked into the compartments of a specially designed stocking box. Beside them lay a few silky thongs, the sight of which sparked a delicious tingle between her legs. Keenan liked to pull the skimpy panties far up over her hips to put a sweet, stinging pressure on her clit. Then he sucked and teased her breasts until she begged for his cock inside her to ease her torment.

If all went as planned, he'd be the one begging tonight.

Next to the lingerie were the educational DVDs Natalie had bought herself: a porn star's guide to oral sex techniques; a set of interviews with committed couples who then made love in front of the camera to lilting New Age music; a sexercise program led by an exotic dancer that culminated in a seductive lap dance. She and Keenan had watched the first two together. He'd been attentive to the expert's cunnilingus tips but amused that all the couples seemed fixated on the outfits they were wearing when they first met. "I was too busy imagining you naked," he said with a wink.

The lap-dance video Natalie had kept to herself. She'd felt too self-conscious to pout and gyrate in front of Keenan. Besides, seductive dancing for her husband felt like something a smooth-voiced doctor would advise to spice up a staid marriage. Her depraved mind had come up with its own prescription, this haunting desire that made her feel hungry and dirty and dizzy all at once.

She knew she could not rest until she tried it.

Natalie let her gaze wander on to the part of the drawer where she kept the gifts from her husband. One Christmas he'd given her a flesh-colored butt plug, modestly sized for beginners. When she was especially "bad," Keenan would bend her over his knee and slide the toy into her exquisitely sensitive back hole. Then he'd spank the plug in deeper, patiently strumming her clit with his other hand until she came in wracking spasms.

He used the delicate feather duster he'd bought at their local couples-friendly sex store for an especially devilish purpose. He'd warm her up by sweeping the feathers over her bare chest and thighs, then "force" her to rub her own clit with the tip of the handle, while he taunted her for being such a horny slut she had to masturbate with a stick. He always stopped her right on the verge of orgasm and took her in some unusual way: seated on their low dresser, bent forward over the bed, standing up against the closet door. She'd be so hot, she'd actually climax from a few brushes of his fingers on her sweet spot.

Tonight she hoped to work the same magic on him.

Natalie felt her pulse quicken. There was so much of their erotic history hidden in this drawer. Sweet, dark couplings, some quite daring for an ordinary suburban couple. So far one thing had always been the same. It was Natalie who submitted to Keenan, opening herself to his voice, his fingers, his cock, probing and filling her. Yet surrender made her feel strangely powerful in a way she could never express in words. Only recently, after fifteen years of marriage, had she gotten the urge to give him the same gift in return. Was that why she could think of nothing else but Keenan on all fours, naked and whimpering in a voice ragged with desire? *More, yes, more, please.*

Suppressing a shiver, she pushed the sex drawer closed with a satisfying smack of resolution.

Scene Two: The Kitchen, at Dusk

I have to do this. I'll be obsessed with it until I do. But will he play along?

Natalie gave the simmering lentil soup a stir and unwrapped the selection of cheeses she'd bought at their favorite gourmet shop. Dinner would be quick, no lingering over wine, although she lusted for the swaggering courage of a glass of cabernet. She quickly reminded herself that she needed all her wits about her. After all, she'd be the one directing the show tonight.

Keenan had been a good role model in that respect. He had definitely gotten more experimental in the past few years, suggesting sexual acts that first shocked then thrilled her. Was she finally catching up? Of course, he might flat out refuse to submit to her. Yet she hoped that if she could guide him to the place she loved so well, where thought dissolves into pure carnal pleasure, any lingering shame that it was unmanly would melt away.

As she sliced the phallic-looking baguette, Natalie remembered when this troubling obsession began—to the day. It was about a month ago, when her husband had been working from home. They skipped lunch for a shower together, and Natalie playfully soaped up his body, almost accidentally letting the bar of Ivory slide down between his asscheeks. His mischievous smile made her bolder, and she pushed the edge of the soap deeper, rubbing it back and forth in the crevice as if she were fucking it.

He closed his eyes and tilted his head back into the shower's spray.

"Turn around and put both hands on the wall."

Natalie wasn't sure where that commanding voice came from—her own throat apparently. Keenan's eyes shot open in surprise, but he obeyed, placing his large palms flat against the tile as instructed.

"Spread your legs wider," she told him.

He complied without a peep of protest.

Her hands wandered over his backside freely, stroking his thick, strong thighs; raking slippery fingers over his tensed buttocks, hard as iron. But when her finger somehow found its way into his valley, she faltered, caught off guard by the tender, silky flesh. Even more surprising was her husband's deep sigh of response. Her chest tightened. As if she'd crawled into his skin, she felt the electric shudder of being touched in this forbidden place, a witch's brew of shame and pleasure.

Taking a deep breath, she gingerly sought out his tight opening, tracing the rim with her fingertip. At the bottom of the oval, she found a little knob of flesh and instinctively flicked it. Keenan's knees buckled and he moaned, a ghostly countertenor. She'd never heard that sound before from his lips.

Too flustered to go farther, she pulled her hand away, although she burned to explore him in her fingertips, in her belly, in her heart now pounding in its cage.

Released from her wicked spell, Keenan turned and kissed her hard, squeezing her buttocks as if to reclaim his sovereign right. "I should fuck you in the ass for that, you naughty little brat," he growled. But he didn't carry through on the threat. Instead he dragged her straight to bed and they coupled quickly, savagely, in the time-honored missionary position, soaking the pillow with her dripping hair.

Since that day, Natalie had been obsessed with replaying the scene. But this time she would not stop before she was fully satisfied.

The key turned in the front door. Keenan was back from dropping Sophia and her friends off at the movie theater.

This is it. You can't lose your nerve now.

Her lips lifted into a smile. The games were about to begin.

Scene Three: In Bed, with the Lamp On

While Keenan was in the shower—to "freshen up after work," as she suggested with a smile—Natalie put on the whore's-red stockings and matching satin thong. Tugging it high on her hips to get a buzz going, she slithered under the covers of their marital bed.

Her husband walked into the bedroom naked, his skin glowing pink, his penis already bobbing to attention. He smiled down at her and narrowed his eyes.

He obviously thought tonight would be like every other time.

Natalie played along at first, letting him kiss her and murmur approval when his wandering hands discovered the lingerie.

Then she pulled away. "I want to have my way with you tonight."

He grinned. "You always do."

"No, this time I have something specific—and rather different—in mind." She was pleased to note that her voice was flawlessly steady and assured.

Keenan lifted his eyebrows. "What did you have in mind?"

"You'll find out soon enough. But don't worry. The second you beg me to stop, I will."

Now he looked a bit afraid.

"Can't handle your own medicine?" Natalie teased.

"This isn't like you." His smile drooped with a touch of uncertainty.

"That's the point, isn't it? But enough discussion, darling.

Now get on your hands and knees. Head down on the pillow, ass in the air just like I do."

"Nat, what are you up to?"

"Do it."

In spite of her doubts earlier in the day, it proved that easy to get her proud, and, if truth be told, somewhat arrogant husband just where she wanted him.

Kneeling behind him, she hiked the thong up higher so the string bit voluptuously into her labia. The sensation reminded her of the way she used to masturbate in college, kneeling beside her bed and flinging one leg up onto the mattress so she could rub herself on the edge. Hard as it was to believe, she'd been too shy to touch herself with her fingers.

How far she'd traveled since then.

Natalie studied her husband, now bent forward in a classically submissive—and revealingly vulnerable—pose. In the golden lamplight, she could see the fine, graceful whorls of damp hair framing his delicate pink skin. She felt a clutch in her belly, lust mixed with fear. Could she actually do this in real life? Lean over and kiss him there on that delicate mouth? In her erotic reveries, she had him groaning at first touch, but what if he found her virginal efforts awkward, laughable? Keenan had rimmed her several times, reduced her to jelly, in fact, but she'd never thought to take notes on technique. Not to mention, this act was the very antithesis of wifely duty. Throughout history, men troubled by such a decadent desire had doubtless been forced to turn to a professional for satisfaction.

She noticed Keenan's body was trembling slightly as he awaited her next move.

There would be no more waiting.

She squeezed her eyes shut and bent forward. In the darkness, she was suddenly aware of the intense heat radiating from his body. She leaned in farther, breathing in soap mixed with his intimate male spice, a surprisingly innocent smell.

Do it. Now.

Eyes still closed, she extended her tongue and pressed it to the puckered orifice.

Keenan gasped.

Her tongue swirled in a full circle.

He let out a groan.

This was quite fun, she thought, rather like playing a musical instrument.

She sought out the little knob of flesh. It felt somehow larger against the tip of her tongue than when she'd touched it with her finger.

Again that strange, ghostly cry of pleasure filled the room, and Keenan choked out an "Oh, god."

Natalie flicked her tongue back and forth a few more times to drive her point home, then pulled away.

"Do you like this, darling?" she asked in sugared tone.

Keenan stuttered a yes.

"I must confess I like it, too. I like having you on your knees and doing to you exactly what you do to me. Now I know what it feels like to be you, and you know what it feels like to be me."

Keenan groaned, in agreement or ecstasy, she wasn't sure.

She smiled. "Since we have such an equal marriage now, if you want me to keep doing this, you have to do something for me. While I cozy up to your back door, I want you to wank your willie. But don't you dare make a big mess on our bed. If you ever have the slightest urge to shoot, stop and take a deep breath. Then start wanking again. Can I trust you to be a good boy and do as you're told?

"Yes, I'll be good," he croaked.

"Then go ahead and get started on your assignment."

Keenan brought his hand to his shaft and began to tug. The bed shook faintly, rhythmically.

Natalie felt her own body tremble, too. All day she'd worried that she'd be too scared or squeamish, but her biggest hurdle now was her own arousal.

You're in charge. Do it.

She dropped her hands to the bed to steady herself. This time, her tongue found his sweet spot like an old friend. She teased him mischievously, brushing it with the tip of her tongue, blowing on it softly, then taking another trip around the taut, puckered ring. Keenan's thighs shook and his breath came in melodious gasps. She could feel his fist moving more slowly to compensate. He was being a very good boy indeed.

In contrast, Natalie quickened her attentions, licking him up and down with the flat of her tongue, lapping the edges of his valley as she might savor a cup of gelato with a doll-sized spoon.

It was then that the strangest image popped into her head: a small pink change purse she'd bought in Chinatown long before her marriage. The purse was impractical, holding no more than a dozen coins, but it was so cute, so mysteriously *foreign*, she liked to hold the little pouch in her hand until the satin grew as warm as her skin. Then she'd slip her finger through the drawstring and stroke the coins. They added up to little more than a dollar, but to her this coin purse had magical powers. It could transform ordinary money into fairy's gold, a currency that could buy the most precious, priceless things on earth.

Perversely, this sentimental recollection filled Natalie with a lewd new hunger. This hadn't been part of her fantasy, but she wasn't about to lose her nerve this time. Fearlessly, she pressed the tip of her tongue to his pink satin purse and pushed it in a few millimeters. The walls were tight but elastic, the flavor faintly metallic. Her pussy throbbed in empathy.

She commenced a series of shallow, stabbing motions.

Keenan's hand dropped from his cock, and he collapsed onto the mattress. "Stop, oh god, I'm going to come all over the bed if you don't stop."

With an exultant smile, Natalie sat back on her heels. This act was supposed to be degrading—"brown-nosing" was not a pretty word—but instead she felt a rush of power surging through her body. Was it that she had "known" her husband in a hidden, vulnerable place, breaking several taboos along the way?

"Well, I did promise I'd stop," she said coolly. "But I'm not done with you. Turn over on your back and use that rock-hard boner you have from my ass-licking to fuck me. Don't you dare come until you've pleased me well."

Still panting, Keenan rolled over and waited compliantly for her to swing a leg over him. Natalie pulled aside the thong and sank down onto his cock. Unable to restrain a moan of pleasure, she rocked against him hungrily. Without further instruction, her husband began his multitasking magic that always brought her to orgasm quickly: nursing one breast and twisting the other nipple between his fingers, all the while tickling her anus through the thong with a dancing forefinger.

Natalie arched her back and thrust her pubic bone into his hard stomach. The tingling between her legs gained force, surging up into her belly as a ball of red-hot flame. On cue, Keenan's finger burrowed under the thong strap and sank knuckle-deep into her anus. The fireball exploded, hurtling her up into space, then easing her down with a series of contractions that made her hips buck like a bull rider's.

Afterward, Keenan gazed up at her, his eyes glowing. "You're priceless."

Hooking his hand around her neck, he drew her gently forward and kissed her deeply.

"By the way, I'll let you come now," she murmured when their lips parted. "But only if you're a good boy and keep thinking of the wicked thing I made you do."

"Oh, I'll be a very good boy," he said with an impish smile. Grabbing her hips, he began to thrust up into her, slowly, as if he meant to take a long time.

Relaxed and fully satisfied, Natalie closed her eyes to enjoy the ride.

ABOUT THE AUTHORS

KRIS ADAMS writes short fiction, fan fiction, poetry and erotica. Her work has appeared in *Best Women's Erotica 2009, Best Lesbian Romance 2010, Girl Crush* and *Daily Flashes of Erotica*.

JANINE ASHBLESS has had five books of erotica published by Black Lace. Her short stories have been published in many Cleis anthologies including *Best Women's Erotica 2009* and *2011, Best Bondage Erotica 2011* and *Fairy Tale Lust*. She blogs about Minotaurs, Victorian art and writing dirty at janineashbless.blogspot.com.

HEIDI CHAMPA (heidichampa.blogspot.com) has been published in numerous anthologies including *Best Women's Erotica 2010; Please, Sir; Orgasmic* and *Alison's Wonderland*. She has also steamed up the pages of *Bust* magazine. If you prefer your erotica in electronic form, she can be found at Clean

Sheets, Ravenous Romance, Oysters and Chocolate and The Erotic Woman.

KARENNA COLCROFT is a former schoolteacher who now writes full-time, when her muse allows it. She has been published by several e-publishers, including Pink Petal Books, Ellora's Cave and Siren. Karenna lives in the northeastern United States with her two daughters and her real-life romance hero husband.

ELIZABETH COLDWELL lives and writes in London. Her short stories have appeared in numerous anthologies including *Please, Sir; Smooth* and *Orgasmic*. She can be found blogging at The (Really) Naughty Corner, elizabethcoldwell.wordpress.com.

JUSTINE ELYOT is the author of full-length erotica titles *On Demand* and *The Business of Pleasure*. She has a range of shorter stories available from Total E-Bound, Black Lace, Cleis Press, Xcite Books and Noble Romance. Her double life is lived in the UK.

A. M. HARTNETT published her first erotic short in 2006. She lives in Atlantic Canada and has set most of her work in this locale. For more information on her publications, please visit amhartnett.com.

KAY JAYBEE wrote the erotic anthologies *Quick Kink 1, Quick Kink 2* and *The Collector*. A regular contributor to oystersand-chocolate.com, Kay also has stories published by Cleis Press, Black Lace, Mammoth, Xcite and Penguin. Details of her work can be found at kayjaybee.me.uk.

DELILAH NIGHT is an American living in Singapore with her husband and young child. Besides erotica, she writes about sex after parenthood and sex-positive parenting. In time, Delilah hopes to be a licensed sexologist and sex educator. She invites you to visit her website, delilahnight.com.

KATE PEARCE spent much of her childhood living very happily in a dream world. A move to the USA finally allowed her to fulfill her dreams and sit down and write her first romance novel. Kate is published by Signet Eclipse, Kensington, Ellora's Cave, Cleis Press and Virgin Black Lace/Cheek.

TIFFANY REISZ's first novella, *Seven Day Loan*, came out as a Spice Brief in December 2010. Her first full-length novel is *The Siren*.

COLE RILEY is the author of several street classics, including *Hot Snake Nights, The Devil To Pay, Rough Trade, Harlem Confidential* and *Guilty As Sin*. He is the editor of the Cleis Press anthology, *Making The Hook-Up: Edgy Sex with Soul*. He lives in New York City.

Despite a fear of heights, **CRAIG J. SORENSEN** has been known to scale predatory trees, au naturel, since he was young. His erotic fiction, another means of climbing, has appeared in numerous anthologies and publications worldwide.

DONNA GEORGE STOREY is the author of *Amorous Woman*, a steamy novel about an American woman's love affair with Japan. She's also published over a hundred literary and erotic stories in such places as *Best Women's Erotica, Penthouse, Passion* and *Fast Girls*. Read more of her work at DonnaGeorgeStorey.com.

ALYSSA TURNER's writings address a woman's desire to really have it all—including the things she's not supposed to want. Her publishing credits include "Two For One" in *Best Women's Erotica 2011*, edited by Violet Blue; "Bittersweet," Xcite Books e-publication, and "Criminal Behavior," a Mainstream Erotica monthly finalist.

ABOUT
THE EDITOR

RACHEL KRAMER BUSSEL (rachelkramerbussel.com) is a New York–based author, editor and blogger. She has edited over forty books of erotica, including *Women in Lust, Obsessed, Gotta Have It; Best Bondage Erotica 2011* and *2012; Her Surrender; Obsessed; Orgasmic; Bottoms Up: Spanking Good Stories; Spanked; Naughty Spanking Stories from A to Z 1* and *2; Fast Girls; Smooth; Passion; The Mile High Club; Do Not Disturb; Tasting Him; Tasting Her; Please, Sir; Please, Ma'am; He's on Top; She's on Top; Caught Looking; Hide and Seek; Crossdressing* and *Rubber Sex.* She is the *Best Sex Writing* series editor, and winner of 5 IPPY (Independent Publisher) Awards. Her work has been published in over one hundred anthologies, including *Best American Erotica 2004* and *2006; Zane's Chocolate Flava 2* and *Purple Panties; Everything You Know About Sex Is Wrong; Single State of the Union* and *Desire: Women Write About Wanting.* Most recently, she served as senior editor at *Penthouse Variation,* and wrote the popular "Lusty Lady" column for The *Village Voice*.

Rachel is a sex columnist for SexisMagazine.com and has written for *AVN*, *Bust*, Cleansheets.com, *Cosmopolitan*, *Curve*, The Daily Beast, Fresh Yarn, TheFrisky.com, Gothamist, Huffington Post, Mediabistro, *Newsday*, *New York Post*, *Penthouse*, *Playgirl*, *Radar*, *San Francisco Chronicle*, *Time Out New York* and *Zink*, among others. She has appeared on "The Martha Stewart Show," "The Berman and Berman Show," NY1 and Showtime's "Family Business." She hosted the popular In the Flesh Erotic Reading Series (inthefleshreadingseries.com), featuring readers from Susie Bright to Zane, and speaks at conferences, does readings and teaches erotic writing workshops across the country. She blogs at lustylady.blogspot.com.